THE PHENOMENALS

A TANGLE OF TRAITORS

F. E. Higgins has been fascinated by the macabre ever since seeing a ghostly apparition as a child. Nowadays Higgins travels the lands, collecting strange artefacts and the even stranger stories behind them. Her Tales from the Sinister City series has sold all over the world.

When not in pursuit of a story, Higgins may be found in a haunted house in Kent.

THE PHENOMENALS

A TANGLE OF TRAITORS

F.E. HIGGINS

MACMILLAN CHILDREN'S BOOKS

First published 2013 by Macmillan Children's Books
a division of Macmillan Publishers Limited
20 New Wharf Road, London N1 9RR
Basingstoke and Oxford
Associated companies throughout the world
www.panmacmillan.com

ISBN 978-0-330-50755-4

1 3 5 7 9 8 6 4 2

A CIP catalogue record for this book is available from
the British Library.

Printed and bound by CPI Group (UK) Ltd, Croydon CR0 4YY

To Violée and Flammando

CONTENTS

Lurid   /ˈloo-rid/ **n.** Supermundane entity. Lurids are the restless shades of executed convicted criminals, often found where the bodies are discarded after death

Phenomenal   /fuh-ˈnom-uh-nal/ **n.** Supermundane entity. Generally malevolent in nature, requiring expert handling to banish, destroy or neutralize. Phenomenals are particularly vile and are characterized by their tendency to gather in small groups and their ability to come and go unnoticed

See also *Lemures, Vapids, Noctivagrantes,* et al.

CHAPTER 1

THE HUNTER

The lucent moon cast her benign light across the glittering roofs of the northern city, and in that gentle light the frosted verges of the Great West Road gleamed eerily. An echoing chime announced the impending arrival of 12 Nox. And marking each chime, like a macabre pendulum, a decaying skeletal form swung to and fro on the ancient gibbet at Quadrivium Crossroads. Thus justice had been served.

Approaching this strangely affecting sight was a girl in a black leather paletot coat. Without hesitation she climbed the seven steps up to the platform and went straight to the body. She steadied it with her hand and looked up at the face. The features were unrecognizable; the local corvids had picked the flesh down to the bone.

'Domna,' she murmured, wrinkling her nose at the smell. 'It's not just the birds that have been at you.' She lifted the sleeve of his left arm. His hand was gone, severed neatly at the wrist. From the way his trousers flapped, she could tell that his left leg was also missing. 'Silvan beluae?' she wondered, and looked over her shoulder at the dark forest some miles distant from the city. 'But they rarely leave the woods.'

She jumped down from the platform, her thick-soled boots leaving a deep impression in the dirt, and was walking away when she saw two men come shuffling up to the gibbet. They were pushing a long, narrow handcart. They too climbed the steps and, as one sawed through the thick rope, the other stood ready to catch the body. It rattled as it fell and its skull snapped off and rolled on to the platform.

'What was his crime?' she asked.

Both men started at the sound of her voice. 'Thievery and murder,' said the man with the knife, peering down from the platform at what he took for a blond youth. 'Robbed a perfumer's and killed an Urban Guardsman.'

'Could do with some perfume now,' joked the second man.

Together they took the body and dumped it unceremoniously on to the handcart. The girl flinched. Even a criminal deserved a little more respect than that. She caught up with them as they started to wheel the cart away.

'Where will you take him?'

'To the Tar Pit. That's where they all go. Best place for 'is kind. Nany graveyard'll have 'im.'

The men hurried off one way and the girl watched them for a while before going in another. Her manuslantern swung back and forth at her side, casting an orange glow. She walked quickly, purposefully, the city lights twinkling behind her. The road was rutted, and the verges lined with ragged bushes and trees.

Shortly she came to two imposing granite pillars, once a magnificent gateway but now showing signs of dereliction. The stone arch that had spanned the gap between them lay nearby broken in two. The girl passed between the pillars and veered off to the left. The landscape changed, stretching away from her darkly, and the ground underfoot was no longer firm. Pools of water reflected the shining moon, and above a myriad blue lights flitted around, tempting her to follow them. But she maintained her path.

'You won't catch me out,' she said, laughing. 'Nany Puca will get me tonight!'

She continued, trying to ignore the constant howling that filled the air, to a set of iron railings. She followed them round to a pair of gates, rusted off their hinges, and as she passed between them she read the words wrought into the iron:

DEGRINGOLADE KOMATERION

In the adumbral komaterion the air of abandonment was tangible. Mossy headstones and statues were barely visible above the tall grass. The girl walked on, stumbling occasionally, until she came upon a small dark building almost completely hidden in the undergrowth and covered in thick ivy. Its wide door was flanked by two columns which supported a pediment in the classical style. This was a kryptos, a building within which lay the bodies of the dead.

The girl took a large key from her pocket, unlocked the door and entered the musty tomb.

'Well, Folly,' she said to herself, 'home, sweet home. At least for now.'

Chapter 2
The Thief

'Spletivus!' oathed Vincent, with justifiable feeling, as he watched the triangular piece of stone fall to the ground some fifty feet below him. It shattered. Only moments earlier his entire body weight had been supported by those fragments.

He laughed lightly at the near miss; it was not the first in his young life. As he continued to inch along the crumbling narrow ledge that ran across the front of the house he exhaled slowly and deliberately. He was not a stranger to precarity, but his current position was more precarious than most. He was four floors up; if he fell he too would shatter like that stone and be dead for sure. He wondered how many seconds it would take before he hit the ground.

But he had no intention of falling. There was a balcony to his left by which he planned to make good his escape through the house. Then the unmistakable sound of a sash window being thrown up caused him to reconsider. Out of the corner of his eye he could see a man craning his neck through the window. He groaned. 'Constable Weed.'

'We've got you this time, lad,' crowed the uniformed man triumphantly. 'You might as well give up now.'

Vincent looked to his left. Now there was another constable on the balcony. He stood at the railing with his arms crossed over his chest. 'It's the end of the line for you, sonny,' he said. 'The Pilfering Picklock will be no more.'

Vincent grinned. 'If you want me you'll have to come and get me.'

Both men frowned. 'You've got nowhere to go,' said Constable Weed. 'Don't be a fool. Come back.'

Vincent laughed. 'To face the hangman's noose? Not a chance, gentlemen.'

He took a small grappling hook on a rope from under his long cloak and tossed it expertly on to the balcony, causing the constable to step back rapidly. He yanked sharply on it, pulling it back and securing it to the balusters. Then, before the disbelieving eyes of Constable Weed and his gape-mouthed companion, Vincent jumped out from the ledge to swing back into the house through the window below the balcony. He landed in a shower of glass but, cat-like, on his two feet. He brushed down his cloak and looked around.

He was in a large bedroom. The occupant of the four-poster bed in the centre of the room, around which were pulled heavy curtains to keep out the winter's cold, had been snoring loudly. Not any more. A fat nightcapped head appeared from behind the drapes.

'Evening, my good fellow,' said Vincent.

'What the . . . ?' spluttered the man, but Vincent dazzled him with a beam of light from a device he had concealed in his hand. Then he raced to the door, opened it as wide as it would go and promptly hid behind it. The two constables came running in at the same time as the man emerged from his bed.

'We're after the Pilfering Picklock,' shouted Weed. 'He came into your room.'

'Good Lord! Then I think he just ran out again,' said the man, still blinded by the flash of light and the fact that he had drunk rather more port than was good for him that evening.

'Search every niche, every nook and every cranny in the house,' ordered the other constable.

So all three – the woozy sleeper and the two constables – hurried from the room to join other members of the household, which included a number of servants whose irritation at being disturbed from their sleep was tempered rather nicely by the fact that their rich and less-than-generous employer had become the latest victim of the notorious thief.

The Pilfering Picklock himself waited until the syncopated footsteps faded, before pushing the door shut. With a practised eye he glanced around the spacious room. On the nightstand there was a crystal glass with a good two inches of red wine in it. He helped himself, of course, to the diamond cufflinks that sat next to the glass and slipped them into one of his many pockets. There was a gilded dressing mirror in a corner of the room and Vincent caught sight of himself. He pushed back his hood, smoothed down his cloak, bulging as it was with spoils, and ran his hand through his thick dark hair. He smiled his winning smile.

'Vincent, you are a handsome fellow, no doubt!'

Then, aware that time was of the essence, he poked his head out into the corridor. A solitary gaslight glowed gently further down the hall. He could hear a medley of excited voices, but they were safely distant. He crept along the hall and skipped lightly down the stairs, three flights in all, sliding down the final banister (oh, they knew how to polish treen, these servants) and hurried to the front door. It was chained and bolted and locked and the key was gone.

'Ha,' laughed Vincent softly. 'No doubt in my honour.'

He took from his belt what looked like a pair of long black pins. Seconds later the lock was picked and he was out on the street. He glanced up at the hook and rope with regret. He hated to lose any of the tools of his trade, but sacrifices had to be made. He walked quickly away from the house and, when a large barrel-laden wagon passed by, stepped into the road and hailed it. The driver looked him up and down.

'Any chance of a ride?' asked Vincent, and flashed his smile. 'I can pay.'

The driver, a ruddy-faced fellow with big hands, mumbled something which Vincent took as a yes.

'Splendid,' he said cheerfully, and climbed up. As he settled into his seat he saw a copy of the local newspaper. And there in black and white on the front page was a head and shoulders portrait of a boy hardly recognizable as himself. The artist had had no choice but to draw him with his black hood up and his eye-mask. He smiled at the headline:

Constables Yet to Capture the Pilfering Picklock

'Definitely time to move on,' decided Vincent. When the local newspaper had gone so far as to bestow a name on you, it was a sure sign that you had outstayed your welcome. And he knew he had been lucky tonight. Weed had been just a little too close for comfort. He turned to the driver.

'Where are you off to?'

'Eastwards,' he replied vaguely.

'The further the better,' said Vincent.

Vincent sighed deeply. The further the better had turned out to be significantly further than he had thought. For six days and nights now they had been travelling. The temperature had dropped considerably, the landscape was barren and the driver had proved to be a rather dull conversationalist who spent most of his time snoozing at the reins. So, when Vincent saw a city in the distance, he poked the driver and halted the horse.

'Where are we?'

'On the border of Antithica province,' replied the driver. 'But I ain't crossing it. That city yonder, that's Degringolade – the City of Superstition they call it. Won't take you more'n a day or so, walkin'.'

Vincent looked again at the distant city. The sun was rising behind it and it sparkled with light, as if it had been sprinkled with glitter. He had heard of Antithica province but knew little about it. As far as he was concerned, any place where he wasn't known held new opportunities.

'I want to go into Antithica,' he said decisively.

The driver shrugged. 'I ain't stopping you. But I'm warning you, it's like a foreign country; they do things different there. It's all card-spreaders and charms and who-knows-what.'

'Thanks,' said Vincent, and tossed a small paper packet to the driver, who opened it and smiled broadly at the pair of pearl earrings sitting in the fold. He looked up to thank Vincent, but he was already striding off down the road.

Chapter 3
The Apprentice

Citrine Capodel went to the French windows and pulled back the flocculent blue and gold curtains that covered them. She opened the doors and stepped out on to the balcony. It was still Prax but already dark and the cold was invigorating. She propped her elbows on the stone balustrade and gazed up at the early moon, catching its light on her hair.

'I do believe it really does look smaller,' she mused. 'Another few days and it will be as far away as it ever gets.'

Normally she loved to stand out here, but this evening she felt more alone than usual. It was almost a year to the day that she had stood in this same spot and watched her father ride off through the gate. She had waved at him but he had not seen her. Later she found his silver timepiece on the hall table and had taken it and counted the hours all night waiting for him to come back. But he had not returned, and that was the last time she had seen him. Maybe the last time she ever would.

A gust of wind carried the sound of howling to her ears and

Citrine grimaced; the Lurids were loud tonight. Father loved this time of year, especially the winter Festival of the Lurids. For as long as she could remember, they had dressed up – she, Father and Edgar – and masked and gowned they had joined the procession down to the Tar Pit, where the Ritual of Appeasement, the culmination of the five-day festival, took place. How the Lurids howled then!

Lowering her gaze to the frosty rooftops of Degringolade, Citrine's eye was drawn to the gleaming Kronometer in Mercator Square. The Kronometer, the tallest building in the city, stood in the centre of the marketplace, persistently measuring the passing of time. The procession started at its foot. This year the lunar apogee was at 5 Lux, so the procession would start even earlier to reach the Tar Pit in time. Citrine set her mouth in a firm line. She had not thought to spend a second Ritual without her father.

Beyond the square, towards the sea, she could see the top of the lighthouse. This, the second tower of note in the city, stood on a rock in the centre of the broad Flumen River, just where its muddy waters mingled with the Turbid Sea. Its intermittent beam guided ships in and out of the harbour.

Citrine shivered, suddenly aware of the biting cold of the night, and went back inside. She walked about the large room distractedly, picking up ornaments and jewellery and items of clothing only to put them down again. She had known luxury all her life. The Capodels were immensely wealthy, but Citrine knew that possessions were no guarantee of satisfaction. She considered it no more than a stroke of luck that she had been born into wealth; Cousin Edgar, on the other hand, seemed to think that he deserved it. Citrine could not be persuaded of that.

With a soft exhalation she sat at her dressing table and looked at herself in the triple mirror. She pulled a face and shook her wavy russet hair back from her face, revealing the glittering brow pin over her right eye. She had taken to wearing the onyx pin these days, to banish negative thoughts. She wasn't sure that it was working.

She opened the left-hand drawer of the table and took out a stiff envelope. Pulling on the black ribbon that held it together, she shook out some of its contents: newspaper articles, some letters, sketches and depictions. She flattened out one particular newspaper cutting, dated a year ago and read it for the hundredth time. The headline made her stomach flip; it always did.

Hubert Capodel – Kidnap or Murder?

Chief Guardsman Mayhew Fessup of the Degringolade Urban Guard states that he and his men are mystified by the recent disappearance of local businessman Hubert Capodel. Mr Capodel owns Capodel

*Chemicals and employs many Degringoladians at
his manufactory here in Degringolade. The Capodel
family is the wealthiest in the province and the DUG
are working on the assumption that Mr Capodel
has been kidnapped. CG Fessup has admitted that
although there has not been a ransom demand they
haven't given up hope of finding Mr Capodel alive.*

*Edgar Capodel, Hubert Capodel's nephew, has
taken over the running of the Manufactory. He told
the Degringolade Daily he was confident his uncle
would be found, and that he felt it was his duty to
continue with business as usual despite the difficult
circumstances. Prominent city businessman Leucer
d'Avidus, who is currently running for Governor of
Degringolade, has promised to do all in his power
to find Mr Capodel and return him to his family. Mr
Capodel was last sighted on the night of the Ritual of
Appeasement and the DUG are appealing to anyone
who might have seen him to come forward.*

But nanyone had come forward. In fact, as far as Citrine
knew, it was she who had been the last person to see her
father, when she had waved at him. She had been over
the events of that fateful day many times. She was not an
eavesdropper by nature, but when, after supper, she had heard

the harsh exchange of words coming from the study she had instinctively stopped at the door. Edgar and Hubert held very different ideas about how to run the Capodel Manufactory – that was not in dispute – but this row seemed different. It was obvious from the exchange that Edgar had done something to upset Hubert.

Citrine had heard Hubert ask him, in utter dismay, 'Are you stealing from me?'

And Edgar had answered, 'If you keep things from me, how else am I supposed to find out about them?'

And then the row had continued along the usual lines; Edgar complaining that Hubert didn't trust him and wouldn't give him more responsibility at the Manufactory, and Hubert reiterating that Edgar wasn't ready.

And that was when Citrine had knocked and walked in. Of course they had stopped arguing then, but there was a look on Edgar's face that she hadn't seen before.

She had forgotten about the exchange because that was the night Hubert had not come home. When she did recall it some days later she had toyed with telling Chief Guardsman Fessup, but decided against it. It proved nothing, and Edgar would doubtless have made life even more difficult for her if she caused trouble for him.

Decisively Citrine replaced everything in the envelope and put it away. Then she drew the black cloth that covered the mirrors and jumped up. From the drawer in her nightstand she took a green velvet drawstring bag. Then she threw on her long grey cloak and hurried out of the room.

Shortly after, Citrine emerged from the house into a walled courtyard. Passing the stable block she noted an empty stall – 'Good, that means Edgar is out' – and rounded the back of the stables to a derelict lean-to. She lifted the door slightly as she opened it to stop it scraping the ground. Inside, a dark shape under a canvas cover almost filled the space. Citrine pulled away the cover and looked with pride and excitement at her father's Trikuklos. She ran her hand over the polished mudguards and patted the leather dust-hood. It was an intriguing vehicle. Designed around a triangular metal frame, it had three large wheels with angled spokes for extra strength. It was powered by two broad pedalators attached to a covered chain and steered by long handles with soft grips. The hood clipped to a glass weather-screen at the front and folded back like that of a perambulator.

Hubert Capodel had been one of the first people in Degringolade to own a Trikuklos, but now they were a common sight on the streets. Edgar still preferred horses, claiming they required less effort.

Citrine climbed in and put on the gloves and goggles that

lay on the front seat, then pedalated the vehicle out of the lean-to and across the courtyard to the wall. Behind a curtain of ivy there was a small door, which, using a key hidden behind a loose brick, she opened and expertly manoeuvred the vehicle through the narrow space. As soon as the door closed the ivy fell back and her secret exit was hidden again.

With a grin Citrine pedalated away at a frightening speed down Collis Hill. She loved the freedom the Trikuklos afforded her and relished the knowledge that Edgar had no idea how she defied him. In the months since Hubert's disappearance, he had slowly and insidiously restricted her liberty. He hired a stern governess, who accompanied her everywhere and taught her at home. And he forbade her from going to the Manufactory. Edgar's excuse for these draconian measures was that they were for her protection, in case the same thing happened to her as had happened to her father, whatever that might be.

In Mercator Square Citrine steered slowly between the stalls until she reached a black kite wagon set back a little from the main thoroughfare. She put on the brake, climbed down and was about to knock on the wagon door when it opened. A sun-wrinkled, aged lady stood there smiling broadly.

'Citrine, how lovely to see you! I had a feeling you would come.'

'Hello, Suma.'

17

Inside the wagon Citrine took a seat under the window, on a soft upholstered bench, and Suma sat on a spoon-back easy chair opposite. A small stove in the corner radiated welcome heat, a black pipe carrying away the smoke through the roof. Citrine looked around, as she always did, taking in the familiar objects, noting new additions. On one shelf there was a row of five cachelot teeth, each nearly six inches high and exquisitely engraved with scaly fish and octopuses and curling waves in black and brown ink. On another shelf there was a sculpture of a hand, and at the far end an intriguing, if repulsive, leech barometer.

'Cold, though not cold enough for snow, and the leeches tell me rain is coming,' said Suma. 'And how are you, my dear? A difficult week, this.'

'I can't believe it's a year,' said Citrine. 'Edgar is . . . well, as bad as ever. I hardly see him these days – he's always at the Manufactory or at his club. I don't care to see him, if I am honest. Is that a dreadful thing to say? I am not sure he thinks of Father at all. I thought it would be a good night to spread the cards.'

'Of course, but try to calm yourself or it will affect the outcome.'

Citrine loosened the string on the velvet bag and took out a rectangular box made from the blackest Gaboon ebony with inlaid mother-of-pearl stars sprinkled randomly across the lid. Inside it lay a deck of cards in a baize-lined depression. She gave the deck to Suma and the old lady handled them with great care, though they showed all the signs of having been much used. She shuffled them expertly with her gnarled yet nimble fingers. From the bottom of the bag Citrine retrieved four polished dice; one seven-sided, one nine-sided, one eleven-sided and the last thirteen-sided. The facets of the first three were scored with varying numbers of parallel lines. She tossed them on to the table.

'Lucky number three,' she said, counting the visible score lines.

Suma nodded. 'Now the fourth.'

Citrine rolled the fourth die, the facets of which were covered with pictures, and it landed with a large black bird uppermost.

'Corvid spread,' said Suma, and she cut the pack and took the top card. She did this eight times in all, then placed four of the cards face down in a vertical line and two horizontally on either side, in the shape of a bird.

The cards were decorated with intricately drawn scenes – in the top corner of one a three-sided occupied gallows, on another a woman weeping at the feet of a fortune teller, and elsewhere what appeared to be a sacrifice, human or animal it was not possible to tell.

At Suma's nod, Citrine picked two cards from the left wing and one from the body. She set them in a straight line and turned them over. Her face fell instantly. On the first card a pair of coal-black corvids fought over a gold coin; on the second, seven corvids perched on the arm of a gibbet; but the third card was the most distressing. It showed, in graphic and scarlet detail, three hook-beaked corvids with oily black plumage pecking and pulling at the bloody entrails of a dead body.

'The Thief, the Traitor and Death,' ventured Citrine doubtfully. She looked at Suma, who smiled approvingly. 'What does it mean?'

'Remember what I said?' said Suma. 'The art of card-spreading cannot be taught. I can only guide you, and even then there is no guarantee that you will succeed.'

'I see no answers about my father,' said Citrine. 'I'm just not good enough, am I?'

Suma touched her lightly on the arm. 'Citrine, you understand the cards better than most, but there are many ways they can be interpreted. Sometimes, the harder you look for answers, the more questions you throw up. And, remember, some will believe in them blindly, others will heed only the cards that promise good fortune and the rest, like Edgar, will dismiss them altogether.' She looked down at the doom-laden cards before her. 'Only time will tell how these play out.'

Chapter 4
The First Gift

'Spletivus!' oathed Vincent in admiration. '*That's* what I call a clock.'

After nearly a day's walking Vincent was worn out, but his fatigued spirits were invigorated by the sight before him. He stood now in Mercator Square, in the heart of the city of Degringolade, staring up at the magnificent Kronometer. The tower was constructed from thirteen close-set burnished steel columns and the mechanical workings of the clock were clearly visible between them; numerous golden interlocking cogs turned haltingly in alternate directions, and a gleaming black pendulum swung back and forth, hissing as it passed through its wide arc, causing shards of reflected moonlight to shoot off into the night sky.

Inscribed into an angled slab at the base of the tower were the words:

Omnes vulnerant, postuma necat

'"All hours wound, the last kills",' said a voice, causing Vincent to jump. 'Cheerful, eh?'

Vincent turned to see a young boy at his side.

'New to town, are you?'

Vincent nodded, quickly assessing the youth and concluding that he was not a threat. 'And I am confused by your clock,' he laughed, pointing at the clock face. 'The dark tells me that it is evening, but what in Aether is the time?'

Vincent was right to be confused. The Kronometer's face was round and numbered as usual, but it was also divided into four parts. Each part had a large letter – N, L, P and C – and a separate small dial.

'Nox, Lux, Prax and Crex,' said the youth helpfully. 'Night, day, afternoon and evening. In Antithica the light is divided into four segments, Nox being the longest, Crex the shortest. The segment hand has just touched Crex and the dial hand is on six, so it is 6 Crex.

'You mean six o'clock?'

'Nanyone says it like that round here. You'll learn – if you stay, that is.' The youth touched his hand to his left shoulder and hurried off.

'Hmm,' mused Vincent. 'We'll see about that.'

Quickly, unnoticed, Vincent slipped in behind one of the columns of the tower. Instantly he was hidden from view, as he liked to be. He began to climb, using the internal latticework of the structure as rungs, until he was high enough to look down on the marketplace and the surrounding buildings below. He settled in, quite securely, behind the pendulum, disturbing a flock of corvids as he did so. He blew on his hands, the metal was cold, and contemplated his position, both metaphorically and literally.

You could learn a lot about a place when no one knew you were there.

Casting an eye over the city Vincent could see that it was a place worthy of the Kronometer. The buildings were constructed from a curious combination of stone and metal. The rooftops were steeply pitched and were made from brazen sheets of riveted metal rather than tiles. The skyline was a ragged silhouette of domes and steeples, pinnacles and cupolas. Grotesques and gargoyles and dripstones were in abundance under the eaves, and all about decidedly lifelike stone corvids perched in small niches and over windows and doors.

Vincent sniffed. There was a distinct smell in the air, like burning caoutchouc, originating, he decided, from five tall chimneys smoking in the distance. On each chimney were painted three large intertwined letter Cs. But what in Aether was that terrible wailing?

Vincent listened as it came and went, a long haunting

'*Reeeeee*'. Then the wind changed and it faded away altogether, so he looked again to Mercator Square. There were pedestrians aplenty still, making their way home at the end of the day, and horsemen and, to his delight, more than a few Trikukloi. He knew of this novel mode of transport, a vehicle with three wheels rather than four legs, steered and powered by a single person, but he hadn't seen one in actuality. Some said it would soon outdo the horse and cart; others, generally the older generation, sniffed and said that it was not a natural way to travel. Degringoladians were obviously forward in their thinking.

But there's something odd about these people, he thought suddenly. The way they walk down the street, with little hesitations, and how they constantly touch the walls.

Intrigued, Vincent climbed down and stood at the base of the tower. The wailing was audible again, though much quieter, and here he could see better what was going on. The passers-by weren't actually touching the walls; they were brushing small amber projections with their fingers as they passed. And instead of tipping their hats to acknowledge friends or to say goodbye, they gestured to each other the way the youth had to him earlier, rapidly tapping their own left shoulder. Then Vincent nearly laughed out loud. Did his eyes deceive him? This place was a pickpocket's paradise! These people carried their purses in full view.

And he was right. Everyone, young and old, carried small purses of varying colour and size quite visibly, attached by means of a short string to a button on their jacket or cloak.

Vincent, invigorated by the novel and perplexing nature of the city, forgot his exhaustion and took a walk among the maze of booths and stalls in the square. The stallholders were distracted, busily clearing away, and he filched fruit and bread freely as he went with a sleight of hand that came from not just practice but an innate talent. Ribbons of bunting hung between the stalls; black triangular flags painted with ghoulish faces in red bordered with symbols in gold. A leaflet fluttered around his feet and he picked it up.

BE PREPARED, CITIZENS!
ENJOY THE RITUAL OF APPEASEMENT IN SAFETY.
PURCHASE YOUR CRYSTALS AT SALISBURY'S SALARIUM!
LOW PRICES, TOP QUALITY.

Vincent shook his head in disbelief. Crystals? What nonsense was this? He stuffed the leaflet in his pocket and walked on until he found himself at the steps of a black kite wagon. A large corvid perched on the corner of the angled roof and watched him with unblinking eyes. The doors were open, but the curtain behind was closed. Nearby an old sandwich board declared:

SUMA DARTSON
YOUR CARDS SPREAD AND READ
(1 SEQUENTURY)

Vincent laughed softly. Somehow it didn't surprise him to find such a person in Degringolade. His father had had little time for such people, pouring scorn on fortune tellers and table-knockers.

I earn my living from honest thievery, he used to say. *I don't lie to anyone. Those card-spreaders, they look you in the eye, tell you a pack of untruths and still take your money!*

Vincent smiled wryly. What would his father have thought of Degringolade? Above all he had been a practical man. Yes, he would have laughed at the purses on view, but he would not have laughed at the obvious wealth in the city. Together, father and son, they would have stood in the shadow of the Kronometer and planned an evening's work. It was the large houses on the hill they would have targeted, in particular the white mansion Vincent had spotted from on high. Whoever lived there did not lack for money. Vincent flinched as a familiar sharp pain stabbed at his guts. His father wasn't here. He would have to plan and thieve on his own. It was something he was still getting used to.

The corvid suddenly took flight, startling him back to the

present. Something to the side of the wagon caught his eye. A Trikuklos.

Vincent almost rubbed his hands with delight at the sight of the vehicle and immediately went over to examine it. He pressed one of the tyres with his thumb, and the thick rubber yielded ever so slightly. Should be quite a comfortable ride, he concluded, having not yet forgotten the distinctly uncomfortable seat he had endured on his way here. He opened the door and ducked his head in under the hood for a better look. He was thus engaged when he felt a tap on his shoulder.

'May I help you?' asked a quietly sophisticated voice.

Vincent pulled his head out and straightened. A green-eyed girl, perhaps a little older than he, was standing beside him. She was the owner of the machine; that much was obvious from her garb, namely leather high-cuffed gloves, a hat with ear flaps and a pair of large goggles presently hanging around her neck.

Vincent flashed his smile, the one that always charmed. 'Allow me to introduce myself. I'm Vincent Verdigris.'

The girl looked at him coolly. 'I am Citrine Capodel,' she said with that air of confident entitlement Vincent had heard many times before. 'Now, please excuse me. I must go.'

'Your Trikuklos, it's marvellous,' he said, stepping back, but not quite enough, so the girl had to brush past him to

27

climb in. He took great pleasure in unsettling her sort. And in burgling them.

'Kew,' she said politely, and then took off, expertly negotiating the narrow aisles between the stalls.

Vincent watched her go. As soon as she was far enough away he shook her purse out of his sleeve. He loosened the strings and looked inside, to find only greyish crystals. He dipped in a finger and licked it and immediately spat. 'Uurgh!'

'Unrefined sea salt,' said a woman's voice. 'Bitter as bile.'

Vincent looked up, gurning, still trying to rid his mouth of the taste. An old woman was standing on the steps of the kite wagon.

'Suma Dartson at your service. Would you like your cards spread, young man?'

'No, thanks,' he said. 'I don't believe in all that sort of stuff.'

'New here, are you?' she asked with a knowing look. 'I wonder how long before you change your mind. "That sort of stuff" is the lifeblood of Degringolade.'

'Is that so?' Vincent made no attempt to hide his scepticism. He looked boldly at the woman but found it hard to hold her gaze, sensing that she was immune to his smile. 'So what's all this bunting about?' he asked, strangely compelled to break the silence. 'Not exactly cheerful, is it?'

'This week is the Festival of the Lurids,' replied Suma.

'The Ritual of Appeasement is only days away. But you have your salt already. And I have something for you too.' She disappeared inside the wagon.

Festival of the Lurids? It was not a festival Vincent knew. He toyed with the idea of leaving, but Suma was back before he had decided one way or the other.

'Still here?' she asked, as if she knew what he had been thinking. She handed down a linen bag.

Vincent looked inside and his face creased up with disgust. 'A wax hand?'

Suma laughed. 'Make sure to look after it. I'll be asking all about it next time. You never know, even a non-believer like yourself might find use for a Supermundane artefact.' She stepped back into the wagon and pulled the louvred doors closed.

Vincent was rarely at a loss for words, but for a few seconds he stood with his mouth agape. 'Next time? I suppose a card-spreader should know.' Tentatively he reached into the bag and gingerly took out the hand. Modelled on a man's hand, by the look of it, it smelled strongly of herbs, and was so well sculpted that Vincent had almost thought it was real. A short piece of wick projected from the middle finger.

Oh, it's a candle, he realized with a certain amount of relief. Thinking now that it might be useful, or saleable, he dropped it back in the bag and tied it to his belt. Then he took stock of his surroundings: the shining clock tower, the grinning gargoyles, the eccentric architecture, the fluttering black flags.

This has to be the queerest place I've ever been, he decided. But there were rich pickings and the possibility of a Trikuklos to boot! First things first, he had to think business. He patted his pockets; it was time to offload his spoils. There was bound to be a pawnshop or suchlike somewhere.

As luck would have it, across the square, halfway down Hawkers Road, he saw a familiar sign – a spinning gold coin. Vincent smiled broadly; a caveat emptorium. Every city had one of these shops, even as odd a place as Degringolade.

So off he went, whistling a tune that owed more to enthusiasm than skill.

Chapter 5
The Second Gift

'Hello,' called out Vincent, pushing open the door. There was no answer. Gradually his eyes adjusted to the light and he saw that the place was crammed with an uninspiring collection of secondhand odds and ends, including a deep wicker basket of rather worn-looking gas masks. He picked up a rusty metal artificial arm. It was hollow, designed to fit up to the elbow and attach with straps and buckles to the shoulder. Vincent attempted to put it on, but it proved to be trickier than it looked.

'Fully functioning model,' said an arenaceous voice from behind him. Vincent jumped and tried to disentangle himself from the prosthesis. 'It's ingenious,' continued the voice. 'Even the finger joints work – they can lock into place, around a cup or perhaps a dagger. And you can detach the fingers if you don't need them. But you got your two hands, I see.'

Vincent finally freed himself from the tangle of straps. The speaker came into view and it was hardly a pleasant sight:

a carneous man holding a manuslantern which revealed in chiaroscuro his fleshy, florid face, his cauliflower nose, treble chin and small piggy eyes.

'Welcome, young sir, to my Caveat Emptorium. Wenceslas Wincheap at your service. Sumthin' for ever'one, that's what I say.'

To those who knew him well, and they were few, Wenceslas Wincheap was living proof of the unreliability of judgements based on first appearances. He was a man of many talents, but it suited him to keep them well hidden. He continued talking, all the time rubbing his thumb and middle finger together as if trying to get rid of something tacky. 'I sez to meself when I sees yer, there's a boy knows wot's wot. New in town? Have you had your cards spread yet? You're in Degringolade now – nanyone leaves without having his cards spread. Suma Dartson, she's the best, they say.'

'She offered but I declined,' interjected Vincent when the man took a breath.

'You turned down an offer from Suma Dartson? Well, well! Let's hope you don't live to regret it. See over the door there?' Wenceslas pointed to the top right corner of the door frame.

'You mean that ceramic creature with the missing leg?'

'Not ceramic,' corrected Wenceslas. 'Adderstone. It's a

three-legged frog, for luck. Be wary of any house that don't have one. Or any place that don't cover the mirrors at night.'

'Cover the mirrors?'

'You know, to keep the Lurids from stealing your soul.'

Vincent tried not to laugh. These people were slaves to superstition, innocents ripe for the picking. 'I must confess, Mr Wincheap, I don't know what a Lurid is.'

Wenceslas leaned forward conspiratorially. 'The restless dead, my lad. The shades of murderers wot won't settle. There's hunnereds of the filthy creatures in the Tar Pit, down on the old Degringolade estate. Vile place, the tar bubbles like a pot of overdone porridge day and night, and spews out poisonous gas, like stinking belches.'

'Oh, so that's the smell!'

Wenceslas nodded. 'But ever' cloud has a silver lining. The tar lights the city, and powers the Manufactory. Why, it keeps the Kronometer going in Mercator Square. The governor, Leucer d'Avidus, owns the pit. He has pumps working night and day, sucking up the tar, filtering it and stirring it and who knows what else. One day it'll run out and then he won't be so smug.'

'And that's where the, er . . . Lurids are?' said Vincent, bringing him back to the point.

'Oh yes, and they ain't happy! They floats about the pit with evil still in their rotten, murderous hearts. But they're trapped, surrounded by the salt marsh. Salt burns 'em like fire.'

'The purses of salt,' murmured Vincent. It was all starting to make sense now.

'You mean Brinepurses. They're full of brine crystals, 'vaporated from the Turbid Sea, for protection from the filthy beggars.'

'But they're trapped.'

'But it's the lunar apogee soon.' Wenceslas saw Vincent's blank expression and explained. 'When the moon is furthest away in its orbit from the earth. You see, the pull of the moon also makes sure the Lurids stay put, but when it's far away its influence is weakened and it's possible a dark-hearted person could set the Lurids free.'

'And how would a person do that?' asked Vincent, deciding to play along.

Wenceslas shrugged. 'Nanyone knows. It's one of 'em secrets lost down the centuries. Anyhoos, at the end of the Festival of the Lurids we all dresses up and goes to the Tar Pit and tosses in offerings – chickens and sheep, a sort of 'pology for keeping them there – then we goes home and feasts.'

Vincent laughed. 'Sounds like an excuse for a shindig.'

Wenceslas looked down at Vincent's belt. 'You mock, but I see you've got yerself a Brinepurse.'

Vincent quickly pulled his cloak together. 'I . . .' he began, but suddenly the door was thrown open and there was an angry shout.

'Wincheap! Where are you, you cheating swine?'

A tall man in a fur-collared cloak was standing in the shop doorway. Instinct – or the glint of silver around the newcomer's neck and wrist – inclinated Vincent to stay out of sight. He shrank back into the shadows and was rendered almost invisible. The man's cloak flapped about his lower legs, revealing intermittently a shimmering green lining. The hood, also trimmed with fur, fell in soft folds upon his narrow shoulders. Rather well-dressed for this establishment, thought Vincent from his hiding place.

Wenceslas, having moved surprisingly quickly, was now at the door. His bulk prevented the man from coming in any further. 'An' a good evenin' to you too, Mr Kamptulicon,' he said coolly. 'Is there a problem?'

'Here's the problem.' Kamptulicon threw a gas mask at Wenceslas's feet. 'It's a dud. I want another.'

Wenceslas stroked one of his chins, causing all three to wobble, and took another mask from the basket. He dusted it off and handed it over.

'This had better work,' said Kamptulicon, 'or I'll be back.' He turned on his heel and strode away.

Vincent stepped out into the light as Wenceslas shut the door. 'Who was that?'

Wenceslas chewed thoughtfully on his lip, all talk of Lurids and festivals forgotten for the moment. 'His name is Leopold Kamptulicon. He has a lamp shop on Chicanery Lane, not far from here, but if that man's a lamp merchant then –' here he looked slyly at Vincent – 'I'll climb the Kronometer and clean the clock!' He sighed. 'I wouldn't trust him as far as I could drag his skinny rump. Anyhoos, lad, it's near closing time. Are you here to sell or buy?'

'To sell.' Vincent rummaged through his pockets and produced a considerable haul (which would have greatly upset Constable Weed) and laid on the counter rings, necklaces, some silver spoons, five silk handkerchiefs and the crystal glass. Wenceslas hummed and hawed and eventually handed over a fistful of coins. They were not like any Vincent had seen before. Wenceslas answered his question before he asked it. 'Sequins, sequarts and sequenturies,' he said. 'The currency of Degringolade. Take 'em or leave 'em.'

Vincent took them and as he added them to his own purse he remembered Suma's present. He showed it to Wenceslas, who didn't seem at all surprised. 'A Mangledore.'

Sounds like some sort of vegetable, thought Vincent. 'Suma Dartson just gave it to me for no reason.'

Wenceslas raised a bushy brow. 'Suma never gives nanyone nanything for no reason. Take my advice: keep it.' He sniffed it before handing it back. 'Quite fresh too.'

'Fresh? You mean it's real?' Vincent dropped it quickly into the bag.

'Oh yes, the severed hand of a hanged man. A lighted Mangledore strikes the sleeping with the afflictions of the dead – they can't see, hear or move as long it stays alight. And it can only be quenched in cow's milk drawn that day. The holder is immune.' He looked at Vincent slyly. 'Very useful if you're in the business of thieving, at night.'

'I think it's time I went,' said Vincent.

'Here, I got something for you too, a sort of welcome to the city.' Wenceslas held out his hand, upon which rested a small polished metal acorn.

'Let me guess,' said Vincent. 'For luck?'

'See?' said Wenceslas with a grin. 'I knew you knew wot's wot!

Chapter 6
The Dark Heart

'My word,' breathed Folly. 'I had almost forgotten. It really is a different world down here.'

She was standing at the top of a steep slope; behind her was the salt marsh, and stretching before her into the darkness was the treacherous Tar Pit of Degringolade. It resembled a vast dark lake, but it was no serene watery surface she gazed upon, far from it. This was a lake of tar: sticky, noxious, black tar, oozing up from deep below the earth. The tar never set, merely thickened and thinned with the passing seasons, and its depth was unknown. In winter it was at its most dense, on account of the cold, and its heaving surface was like a rash of plague boils, each pustule swelling into a fat bubble that strained to its limit before exploding and releasing toxic gases. Mothers warned their children to stay away on pain of death. They knew that once in the tar's agglutinant hold, the chances of escape were virtually nil.

Folly adjusted her gas mask, tightening the straps, but even with the mask filtering the miasma, the acrid air stung her nostrils and caught in the back of her throat. She descended the worn trail and stood on the narrow shore. All about, blackened tapering pillars of salt rose from the ground, like a charred forest, and the shore was strewn with animal skeletons, innocent victims of the gas or the tar. But there were also the bones of the guilty, for this dark slick was the last resting place of scores of convicted criminals, hanged by the neck and then thrown unceremoniously into the pit. The churning tar disgorged its grisly contents on a regular basis, the fleshless remains of those who met their end by the noose carried ashore by the undulations of the viscous soup.

Poor devils, thought Folly, and curled her lip in revulsion. She thought of the body on the gallows. Whether criminals deserved their fate or not – for justice was not an exact science – there was no satisfaction to be had from the sight of their exposed and blackened remains. This place truly was the dark heart of Degringolade.

Folly listened to another noise, not the sucking and popping tar but a low hum and a rhythmical swooshing. She looked across the seething surface towards the far shore, the origin of the noise, and saw a number of large grey pipes rising like metal tentacles from the tar. They stood a foot or so above the lake and then bent at a right angle and travelled parallel to the surface towards the shore, where they entered the side of a pump house. The pump house was attached by the same exiting pipes to a much larger windowless building. Signs on the walls of the building and treen notices hammered into the ground along the shore warned in letters big enough to read even from this side of the pit:

LDTC
LEUCER D'AVIDUS TAR COMPANY
REFINERY AND FILTRATION
NO ENTRY
TRESPASSERS WILL BE PROSECUTED

But Folly wasn't interested in Governor d'Avidus's tar business. She turned her attention back to the pit. A thick mist hung just above the febrile surface some distance from the shore. Folly fixed her gaze on it.

'Well, hello again,' she murmured, and her heart gave a little jump as the swirling haze seemed to separate and *they* came into view. Now she could see that the mist was actually a horde of luminous shadows hovering above the tarry broth. The shadows were flitting from side to side in obvious agitation. The wind brought to her ears their incessant moaning and wailing.

'The Lurids of Degringolade,' she breathed. 'Desperate as ever to be set free!'

As she watched the nebulous Lurids something changed

40

in their behaviour. They stopped their aimless meanderings and all turned to face the same direction – Folly's direction. As one, the group advanced slowly across the pit. Closer and closer came the ephemeral shades, murderers and violent criminals in life, no different in death. Folly felt rising fear but she stood her ground. They came to the very edge of the pit, but no footprints marked their presence, and they reached out with their pale skeletal arms, moaning and wailing like keening at a wake, held back by an invisible force.

Close up, the Lurids of Degringolade were a most terrible sight to behold, with their crooked necks and lifeless eyes, and their earthly crimes reflected in their wretched expressions. There was not a man alive who would not feel repulsed. Folly shivered violently. She could feel their cold touch; she could hear their desperate breaths and smell their stench. It was the stench of vile hearts.

'Free us!' they entreated. 'Free us!'

Folly willed herself to stay calm. She knew the Lurids couldn't harm her; they were trapped in the pit, unable to cross the burning salt marsh, but still her heart beat faster. She steadied her breathing and tried to hold the gaze of the vile faces that lined up before her, clamouring with their gurning mouths. But in the presence of such a ghoulish horde she couldn't help herself and her hand went to her belt and she drew out a curious short-handled three-pronged weapon. She thrust it forward at the hissing, imploring crowd and instantly the Lurids froze. Then, with screams of unexpurgated rage, they turned and fled in distress back to the centre of the boiling liquid. Folly breathed a sigh of relief and replaced the weapon.

There was a sudden movement to her left and automatically she crouched down and scrambled behind one of the salt pillars. Her first thought was that a Lurid had broken free and her hand went again to her weapon, but, no, it was a mere mortal who approached, a tall cloaked man.

The newcomer was making his way awkwardly down the slope, muttering from behind his gas mask. He went straight to the edge of the tar and stared out at the mass of Lurids. Once again they rushed forward, and the man reached into his cloak, revealing a shimmering green lining, and pulled out what looked like a long stick.

Not a stick, a bone, realized Folly. Intrigued and fearful, she waited to see what he would do next. She could not have anticipated the sequence of events that followed.

The man remained at the edge of the tar, leaning forward slightly. The Lurids were distinctly aggravated, and their moans and howls took on a new strained pitch. Unperturbed by his ghostly audience, the man put his hand to his neck and pulled out a pendant on a silver chain. Where Folly would have expected to see a jewel, there was instead a simple grey stone, irregular in shape. He placed one hand over the stone and threw the bone out into the tar. Like starving street curs the Lurids rushed towards it, reaching wildly, but it fell through their fingers and landed softly and began to sink. They hovered menacingly where it had fallen. Folly felt a little shiver run up her spine. No ordinary man, certainly no Degringoladian, would deliberately antagonize the Lurids.

The man was speaking now and Folly strained to hear what he was saying. His voice was rising and falling with deep emotion. A feeling of cold dread came over Folly.

'*Ades Luride, confestim, ere ossis,*' he called out with finality.

Suddenly from the centre of the writhing horde of fiends a single Lurid emerged. It moved quickly towards the shore and as it approached it changed, becoming less nebulous and increasingly opaque, like cooling fat. It reached the edge of the pit and hesitated. Then, to Folly's horror and disbelief, it actually stepped off the tar and stood on the shore directly in front of the man. Quickly she pulled her head in and pressed up against the pillar, her mouth dry with fear.

'*Sequere,*' said the man clearly. And the Lurid followed.

Folly held her breath as the pair, one alive, one mostly dead, passed within feet of her hiding place. She covered her mask filters with her hands because they weren't sufficient to stop the stench. Nauseated, she watched as they climbed the bank, the man ungracefully, the Lurid stepping lightly behind him with eerie ease. It was no longer ghostly in appearance, being more solid now than transparent and dressed in filthy rags. As soon as they were out of sight Folly dug her hand into her pocket and pulled out a Depiction. She unfolded the stiff paper and looked closely at the faded brown image. Despite the creases, there was no doubting that this was the man she had just seen; it was Leopold Kamptulicon.

'Domna!' she breathed. 'He's just freed a Lurid!'

And behind her the pit surged and bubbled in a chorus of approval.

Chapter 7
Revelation

Citrine piloted her Trikuklos through the streets of Degringolade with a degree of recklessness that was most uncharacteristic. Her face was creased into an anxious frown and she was deep in thought. 'Blast and bother it! What terrible, terrible cards! I almost wish I hadn't gone.'

A sudden cry and a violent jarring caused her to brake sharply and look in her mirror. There was a body lying in the gutter beside the Trikuklos.

'Domna!' She jumped down and ran over to the unmoving figure. Oblivious to the mud and detritus on the road she knelt down beside him. 'Are you all right?'

The fellow groaned and then sat up. 'I think so,' he replied. Citrine helped him to his feet, though he seemed more than capable of doing so himself. Once he was upright she was quite taken aback at his height and breadth. He was very much taller than she was and his shoulders were disarmingly broad. Even his own clothes seemed to strain at the seams. He wore a double-breasted dark pea coat with large turned-up lapels and, to Citrine's surprise, the white toggles that fastened it appeared to be made from the teeth of an animal – evidently a very large animal.

On his head he wore a hat that came low down the back of his neck and covered his ears. She could just see the glint of a gold earring through his black hair. His face was in shadow under the deep brim. He began to brush the dirt from his clothes with his large weather-beaten hands, and exposed a jagged tear in his trousers.

'I am so dreadfully sorry,' apologized Citrine, taking a step back. 'It's entirely my fault. I wasn't looking where I was going. I've had such a wretched spread of cards, you understand . . . but, good gracious! Listen to me go on; that's not your fault, of course. Are you injured in any way? I know an excellent physician, Dr Farquhar—'

'No real damage done,' said the fellow, backing off. He spoke slowly, rolling his *r*s, and Citrine now saw that he was not that much older than she. He picked up what looked like a long leather cylinder with a strap, akin to a bowman's quiver, and shrugged it back on his shoulder. 'All my timbers are in order.'

'Your timbers?'

'I mean, I am not hurt.'

'You must allow me to take you home,' she suggested. 'It's the least I can do. I have a Trikuklos.'

He looked at her vehicle and shook his head. 'There's no need, miss. Worse things happen at sea.'

Citrine was a little disconcerted at the lad's apparent lack of concern for his well-being. 'Oh dear, then, please, for my own peace of mind, let me give you a sequentury, as compensation for your clothes. Your trousers are torn, after all.'

'All right, kew very much,' he said after a brief pause, and, head bowed, he allowed Citrine to press a coin into his calloused palm.

'And here's your Brinepurse,' said Citrine, stooping to pick it up from where it had fallen. He reached back to take it and hurried off, covering the ground quickly with long strides.

'At least tell me your name,' she called after him.

'They call me Jonah Scrimshander.'

'I'm Citrine,' she began, but he was already gone. She climbed into the Trikuklos, still a little shaky from the encounter, and realized with dismay that her own Brinepurse was gone. The string had been cut. She looked down the empty street, but then remembered the other boy, the one outside Suma Dartson's wagon and how he had brushed against her. She had thought it odd at the time and now she knew why.

'Why, the cheek of the boy! Pretending to be interested

in my Trikuklos to steal from me.' She tutted. 'So, the cards were right.' She hoped that was the worst of it.

Still mulling over the cards and the collision, Citrine pushed down hard on the pedalators and coasted silently up to the imposing white boundary wall of the Capodel Townhouse. It was one of the largest residences in Degringolade and stood out from the other houses on the hill just as the Kronometer stood out in Mercator Square. She hoped fervently that Edgar was still away. He strongly disapproved of her interest in the cards. As far as he was concerned, card-spreading was not the sort of skill a young lady of her standing should wish to acquire. Rich, educated people did not engage in such practices; they paid others to do it for them. If Edgar found out that she had been to visit Suma there was no telling what he might do. He had once threatened to lock her in her room. It was bad enough being confined to the house, without that as well.

Citrine slipped inside and crept up the servants' stairs to the main hall. It was a large open space with a galleried landing three-quarters of the way around it. The walls were hung with portraits of many generations of Capodels. Citrine looked up at the one of her mother. She did not remember her, she had died when Citrine was a baby, but she had inherited her vibrantly coloured hair and green eyes. Beside it was the most recent portrait, completed just before her father disappeared, of the three of them: Father, Citrine and Edgar. Edgar had the hint of a smile on his face; Citrine knew well that the artist had taken liberties with his sneer.

Citrine worried sometimes that she might be growing immune to the wealth and luxury that surrounded her, taking it for granted. She thought of the sequentury she had given Jonah, the victim of her own carelessness, and felt guilty that she hadn't offered more. She resolved to make it up to him if she ever saw him again. Then she caught sight of a royal-blue caped coat draped over the arm of one of the trio of French upholstered couches that were arranged around the fountain in the centre of the hall. Her frown was replaced with a smile of delight.

'Florian's here!' She hurried down one of the broad corridors towards the drawing room but, hearing raised voices, she drew up short.

The door into the drawing room was ajar and she could see two men inside. Florian Quince, a bespectacled older man, and her cousin Edgar, exquisitely dressed as usual, with a drink in hand (also as usual). Whatever she thought of his character, Citrine could not deny that Edgar was a handsome chap, with a square jaw, narrow nose and elegant brow. His dark hair was always in place and his eyes were an unusually attractive hazel. But there was an ever-present thin-lipped sneer on his face. Edgar had many admirers among the young girls of Degringolade – undoubtedly his wealth added to his attractiveness – but Citrine knew that he was too selfish to pay attention to any of them for long. Apart from himself, Edgar's greatest love was for money.

Edgar was talking stridently, in fact disrespectfully, to Florian. 'Listen here, Quince, you're just the company solicitor. I own Capodel Chemicals now and I run the Manufactory.'

'True,' continued Florian evenly, 'but there are rumours in the city that you are gambling heavily, associating with undesirables and drinking. Your uncle would not have approved.'

Citrine saw Edgar's familiar shrug. 'Rumours! They prove nanything. I have a dozen friends who would say they aren't true. Besides, my private life is nothing to do with the business,' he said. 'And I'll thank you not to come round here and start an argument you can't win. Your time would be better spent sorting out Uncle Hubert's will and handing over my share. Just declare him officially dead and let me claim my rightful inheritance at last.'

Florian smiled knowingly. 'Ah, I wondered when you would come to that.'

So did I, thought Citrine from her hiding place. It's all you've been talking about for the last month.

'Edgar,' said Florian, 'you recall when you promised your uncle to give up gambling and drinking?'

Edgar stopped mid-sip. 'Yes, what of it?'

'Well, I have proof, Depictions in fact, that you were inebriated at the card table in the Bonchance Club only last week.'

Edgar's face darkened. 'Depictions? You mean images of me captured by one of those newfangled machines? Citrine has one. What's it called again?'

'A Klepteffigium.'

'Yes, that's it. Have you two been spying on me?'

'Not I, but a reputable source. And I have been told that all is not well at the Manufactory.'

Edgar snorted. 'Oh, so you believe the word of a disloyal worker and a couple of Depictions over me? I am the rightful heir to the Capodel fortune, including the Manufactory, and I shall do with it as I wish.'

'You forget the condition.'

Edgar stiffened. 'What condition?'

'The condition in Hubert's will that if you gamble, or drink to excess, you will forfeit your inheritance rights for five years. Citrine, naturally, will still inherit her share.'

Edgar paled, visibly shocked.

'Now, as you have reminded me so often, Hubert has been gone the requisite number of days to be declared legally dead. I will submit the papers to the Degringolade Office of Records tomorrow, and then we can meet to read the will.'

'About time.' Edgar took a large draught of his drink and it seemed to calm him somewhat, but Citrine could see that his hand was shaking. He shot a menacing look at Florian. 'Hubert never said that condition was in the will. Domne! You sly old devil. You drew up the will. Did you tell him to do this?'

Florian tapped the side of his nose and smiled. 'Hubert knew his own mind. Of course, I will have to appoint someone to replace you at the Manufactory.'

Edgar's mouth dropped open. 'No! You can't!'

Florian smiled. 'I can and I will. It's only for five years, Edgar. After that we can review the situation. Citrine's money will be put in trust until she is older, but you will both have a very generous allowance and you may still live in the Capodel Townhouse.'

'Get out!' shouted Edgar. 'Get out!'

Citrine was not surprised at the ferocity of his anger. When Hubert had disappeared Edgar had taken over the reins at the Capodel Manufactory with embarrassing zeal, revelling in finally having complete control. Now it was all slipping away from him. No wonder he was so upset.

She hid behind a pillar and saw Florian come out. Moments later she heard the front door close. Then Edgar emerged, his mouth set in a straight line, his jaw taut, clenching and unclenching his fists. He stomped past and Citrine followed him quietly to the hall. He had on his coat and hat.

'Are you feeling all right, cousin?' she asked innocently.

Startled, Edgar whirled around. When he saw who it was he shot her a look of contempt. 'Spread your precious cards if you wish to know how I am,' he said nastily. 'I have an appointment to keep.' And he left, slamming the door behind him.

Citrine drew back the curtain and watched as he climbed into his scarlet Phaeton and clattered out of the gates. She was suddenly gripped by a feeling of doom. She had met her thief. There were still two cards left.

Edgar, what are you up to now? she wondered.

CHAPTER 8
A LUCKY FIND

Outside the Caveat Emptorium, pondering the encounter with Leopold Kamptulicon, Vincent crossed the road and took shelter in the doorway of Claude Caballoux's Horsemeat Shop. He fished in one of his many pockets for his smitelight, tapped it smartly against his leg and instantly it glowed brightly. In this glow – the same glow that had blinded the man almost a week ago – he examined the gas mask he had managed to conceal under his coat despite Wenceslas's close observation. Vincent fully intended to pay a visit to the Tar Pit and to see these 'Lurids' for himself. He was quite sure they could not be anything other than an illusion created by the unusual properties of the tar, or a trick of the light played on the superstitious and gullible citizens of Degringolade. But the smell of tar was real enough.

It's like a pig's head, thought Vincent, turning the mask over in his hand. Indeed, the porcine resemblance was quite striking. He pulled it down over his head and it enclosed his entire face. A wide glass lens covered the eyes, and from the centre projected a long 'nose' at the end of which was an oval filter. There was also a filter on each cheek. The whole contraption was kept in place with a strap that split around the ears and came together again at the base of the skull. Vincent saw that it did not fasten with a buckle, but instead each end of the strap was covered in a wad of rough material. When the two ends were laid on top of each other they formed a tight bond and had to be ripped apart with a degree of force. It was not a method of fastening that he had come across before. Using the fastener he attached the mask to his belt, alongside the pouch that held his treen picklocks. He tapped the smitelight again to extinguish it. It was without doubt the most useful thing he owned, and a tangible reminder of his father, who had given it to him.

Vincent had not forgotten the silver chain around Kamptulicon's neck or the lumps under the fingers of his glove, rings with large stones if he was not mistaken.

Time to find out a little more about Mr Leopold Kamptulicon, he decided.

He set off for Chicanery Lane, but it was not easy to blend in with the other pedestrians. Normally he would keep close to the walls but this proved impossible, mainly because of the amber touchstones. It also became quickly apparent to him that Degringoladians avoided stepping on cracks in the pavement. All this haphazard movement came as second nature to them, but Vincent succeeded only in drawing unwanted attention to himself by bumping into people. Eventually, concentrating hard, he achieved a sort of synchronized gait with the nimble pedestrians. He even began to touch his left shoulder intermittently, in order to blend in further.

Chicanery Lane was reached via a series of ever-narrowing streets leading off a main road that ran south from Mercator Square. Kamptulicon's shop was situated about halfway down the lane, indicated by a sign in the shape of a lantern projecting from the wall.

Leopold
Kamptulicon
Purveyor of
Domestic
Lighting
And All Related
Paraphernalia

The street was not well lit, the lamp posts were spaced far apart and the light cast was too poor to properly illuminate the lane. The acrid smell that pervaded the city was stronger here. And of course there was still that constant wailing.

'I suppose that'll be our friendly Lurids,' Vincent said to himself, laughing.

The area was grimly unattractive and the ongoing festival was not much in evidence. Here and there people had made half-hearted attempts to hang bunting between the lights, but already it was trailing on the ground. Vincent saw that each lamp post had a large oval badge screwed to it, stamped with the letters 'LDTC' – Leucer d'Avidus Tar Company, he guessed.

Vincent peered cautiously through one side of the shop's bow window. On a tiered display within was an assortment of lights of all sizes and shapes – brass lamps, glass lamps, hurricane lamps, candles, candle holders, candle snuffers, rope wicks and plaited wicks, glass globes, frosted globes and etched shades. On the highest tier of the display there were cans of tar, varying in price according to size and quality, but all stamped with the increasingly familiar LDTC logo.

The display was dusty. Cobwebs stretched from handle to handle to spout to wick and back again, like a collection of little hammocks.

Perhaps Kamptulicon has other pursuits to keep him busy, wondered Vincent presciently. The blind was down, the sign turned to 'closed'. The interior was unlit and when he tried the door it was locked. Leopold Kamptulicon was not expecting customers.

Vincent knocked and waited. Neither sound nor movement came from within the shop. He stepped on to the window ledge and reached up to the semicircular fanlight above the door. Sometimes these windows were neglected and came loose, but this was tightly shut. Undeterred, he set about examining the door. There were three locks.

'Mysteriouser and mysteriouser,' he mused. 'What can this Mr Kamptulicon have to hide that requires such cautious security? Shame he didn't reckon on Vincent Verdigris coming to town.'

Vincent opened the pouch of treen on his belt and pulled out two long, narrow pins. He knelt in the shelter of the porch, inserted the pins into each lock and listened with satisfaction as they released one by one. Once inside the shop he locked the door behind him, but unhooked the window arm above, leaving it just loose enough to open from the outside. He noticed a three-legged frog over the door.

'Another believer,' he murmured. 'Now, Leopold, show me your secrets.'

By the glow of his smitelight Vincent could see no reason to think he was in anything other than a light shop. The counter was tidy, if dusty, with a stack of wrapping paper held down by a chunky paperweight. Scattered about the counter were small tins of Fulger's Firestrikes – ignitable sticklets used for lighting fires – and on a shelf behind the counter were more cans of tar. Vincent oathed softly. He wasn't used to coming away from a place empty-handed. He pocketed a couple of tins of firestrikes, just because they were there, and rounded the counter to take some tar. In doing so he tripped on the dog-eared corner of a rug. The rug folded over on itself, exposing a metal trapdoor.

Much heartened by the discovery, Vincent pulled on the ring handle but the trapdoor didn't budge. He looked for hinges – they could be unscrewed – or a padlock, but there was neither, only an irregular-shaped shallow hole stamped into the metal. He sat back on his heels for a minute, thinking. Something in his pocket was digging uncomfortably into his leg. Wenceslas's acorn. He fished it out but to his surprise it was snatched straight from his hand as if by an invisible force and stuck fast to the trapdoor with a loud click. Of course! It was a magnetic lock, which could only be opened by the corresponding magnetic key.

Vincent hoped that Kamptulicon had not taken the key with him but guessed that it would be hidden nearby. He prised off the acorn and pocketed it thoughtfully, then straightened and looked around. The paperweight on the counter stared back at him. I wonder . . . he thought. Hidden in plain sight?

He took the paperweight and placed it in the shallow hole of the metal plate. It fitted perfectly. He gripped it firmly and turned it clockwise. There was a very soft scraping sound and the trapdoor eased, as if the pressure was off. Vincent pulled on the handle again and this time the trapdoor opened noiselessly. He shone his smitelight into the opening and saw a set of stone steps.

Cautiously Vincent descended, his ears alert to every sound, excited but unafraid. He left the trapdoor open; he did not intend to be down there for very long.

The darkness was such that the smitelight revealed the space no more than a foot or two ahead before blackness closed in. The staircase proved to be precipitously steep and the stone steps so perilously narrow that he had to go down sideways one step at a time. The air was cool and smelled strongly of damp. Vincent could hear his every breath. His heartbeat pulsated through his fingers as they walked their way along the wall.

'Spletivus!' he whispered. 'I must be a hundred feet below the city by now!' In fact it was not quite that deep, but darkness has a habit of exaggerating reality.

Finally he reached the last stair and stepped off into a narrow passageway with craggy walls and an uneven floor and low ceiling. He moved ahead haltingly, expecting at any moment to plunge into a yawning chasm or to smack his head on some rocky protrusion. The tunnel led him on, inexorably, towards . . . towards what? He did not know. He turned a corner and sensed rather than saw that the tunnel had widened out into a chamber. In trepidation about what it might reveal, he held his smitelight above his head. His jaw dropped open and he oathed involuntarily.

The chamber walls were shelved from floor to ceiling, and every shelf without exception bowed under the weight of the most fabulous thaumaturgic paraphernalia. Vincent blinked hard. He had a sudden flashback, of his father at his bedside, telling him the tale of a man of magic who lived in an underground room. This chamber could have been that very room. But that was a bedtime story; this was real. Vincent had seen all manner of oddities in his thieving career; he had uncovered people's darkest secrets, the ones they kept locked in cupboards and pushed to the back of drawers, but none of them could possibly come close to what he could see now.

Slowly he turned on the spot. He saw bottles and bell jars and demijohns, their contents grotesque. He saw animal bones and grinning goat skulls, foul-smelling fungi and pungent herbs, dried leathery wings and peacock feathers, rare objects of beauty in a place of frightful sortilege. This was not the workshop of a merciful diviner or benevolent astrologer; this was the secret lair of someone who engaged in troublesome devilry. And not just that – set away from the table was a chair, bolted to the floor, with leather straps on the arms and legs and on the headrest. Its purpose was not difficult to discern: the practice of torture.

After the initial shock of the find Vincent's innate sense of self-preservation took over and he sprang into action. He lit a lamp and began to rummage through the contents of a large table. Its surface was practically hidden, covered as it was with an abundant array of instruments and disturbing appurtenances, some of which caused him to recoil; others he held up and regarded with morbid interest. A short, stout metal cylinder with thin pipes spiralled tightly around the outside caught his eye. It looked a little like a tavern tankard, with a handle on the side. The lidded end was rounded, the other end flat. It was very cold to the touch and was stamped with a manufacturer's trademark. He dropped it into one of the larger pockets of his coat, another visit to the Caveat Emptorium in mind.

As he rummaged, his practised, searching hand unearthed a very small book that was concealed beneath several layers of curious objects. It was written in what he took to be Latin, and not knowing the language he was about to put it back, when on second thoughts he put his foot up on to the table and reached down to the thick heel of his boot. The heel swung out to reveal a hidden compartment he had crafted himself. He pushed the book into the space. It just fitted.

Satisfied that he had taken all that was useful or valuable, Vincent put out the lamp and shone his smitelight around the room one last time. It was then he saw the rectangular cabinet sitting in the shadows against the far wall. It was made of black metal and was humming softly. There was a handle on the front. Vincent went over and pulled on the handle. The door was heavier than he expected and when it opened there was a soft hiss and an outrush of cold air. The interior was cold to the touch, there were ice crystals on all the inner walls, but the cabinet itself was empty. Vincent shivered and closed the door. Then, coat pockets bulging once again with his spoils, he retraced his steps up the tunnel.

What Vincent did not know was that if a trapdoor opens soundlessly one way, then it most probably closes soundlessly the other. And it did, merely moments after he had gone through it, the magnetic lock sliding back into place. To further compound Vincent's plight, two large barrels of tar were rolled on to the trap door, the noise dulled by the rug.

If only Vincent had arrived a couple of minutes later this would not have happened, but chance is a two-way street. Unfortunately for him, Vincent reached the shop only moments after Leopold Kamptulicon had left for the Tar Pit. Although the lamp vendor was out of sight, he was still within earshot. He heard Vincent's knock, went back to investigate and watched the boy break in. He was most surprised, and put out, when he realized that this brazen intruder had discovered both the trapdoor and the secret of the lock. As soon as Vincent went down the steps Kamptulicon slipped back into the shop, closed and secured the trapdoor and reseated the window arm. Then he set off once more on his Lurid business and his unwitting meeting with Folly.

Nobody took advantage of Leopold Kamptulicon and got away with it.

CHAPTER 9
PROBLEMS AND SOLUTIONS

In another part of Degringolade, far away from the luxury of the Capodel Townhouse – where Citrine was mulling over Florian Quince's recent revelations – but close to the underground chamber where Vincent was unwittingly trapped, Edgar Capodel shifted uncomfortably from one foot to the other beside his Phaeton and blew loudly on his cold, soft hands. He didn't like this part of Degringolade.

'Domne, but hurry up,' he urged into the night.

As if in answer to his plea, a polished Troika drawn by three black horses pulled up on the other side of the road. Edgar ran over to it – the carriage door opened and the steps were let down.

'Thank the Lord you're here, sir,' he said as he climbed in.

'And good evening to you too, Edgar,' replied a smooth voice from the tenebrous interior. The carriage lights were low and the man sitting opposite Edgar was a mere shadow. 'Would you care for some Grainwine?' he asked, taking an elegant bottle of transparent liquid and two glasses from a small cabinet built into the back of his seat. 'You see, I have put your idea to good use.' The cold air within the cabinet rolled out and the atmosphere in the carriage became distinctly cooler.

Edgar nodded.

'You seem troubled,' said the man.

'I am!' replied Edgar, and gulped down a mouthful of the chilled yet burning liquid. 'It's Florian Quince, sir, the interfering old maggot. He says he has some of these "Depictions" and that they prove I was at the Bonchance Club drinking and gambling.'

'And this means what?' enquired the other man.

Edgar hesitated. 'There's a condition in the will. I cannot inherit for five years.'

The silence was brief but meaningful. 'Then we need a new will. What about the Capodel Manufactory? Are you still in charge?'

'Not if Quince has his way.'

There was another silence, broken only by the sound of liquid being poured into a glass.

'I've been stitched up and left out in the cold,' complained Edgar bitterly. 'Expected to live on an allowance, for Aether's sake. And our plans—'

'Stop snivelling, you fool,' hissed the shadowy companion, displaying the first sign of anger. 'You should have been more careful. You know how Hubert felt about gambling. How many times do you have to be told?'

Edgar quailed at the rebuke, and noticed, not for the first time, the man's verbal eccentricity: how he omitted the *b* in gambling, pronouncing it 'gamling'.

'I didn't know what was in the will!' he protested.

'Quiet! I need to think.'

Edgar sniffed and drank.

Then the man spoke. 'This is problematic but not insuperable. But I need you to help with the will.'

'Yes, yes, of course, just tell me what to do,' said Edgar. 'And then there is Citrine. I've done what you said, and kept an eye on her, but she still believes that Hubert might be alive. She won't rest until they find his body.'

'Then let them find a body. We cannot allow Citrine to stand in my . . . our way.'

'But . . . how?'

'Leave that to me. Dr Ruislip, down at the morgue, owes me a favour or two. First things first, the will. I have a plan that can kill two birds with one stone.'

CHAPTER 10
THE WHITE HAIR

'What are you doing in the safe?'

Edgar was kneeling in front of the drinks cabinet which Citrine knew was actually a small safe. He started at the sound of her voice and stood up to see her in the doorway.

'Nany of your business,' he retorted, his eyes flicking to her green bag before she could conceal it. 'Looking into the future again?' he mocked. 'I don't need the cards to tell me what to do.'

Citrine came fully into the room. 'They don't tell me what to do; they guide me . . .' she began, but she knew not to continue the conversation.

'Why aren't you in bed? It's already Nox. Memories keeping you awake, I suppose.'

'You woke me, slamming the front door. You're wearing your coat. Are you going out again?'

'How perspicacious of you.' Edgar's handsome face was easily disfigured by his curled lip. 'Why, are you going to tell Florian, you little spy?'

'How could I spy for Florian when I am practically a prisoner in my home? Actually I'm looking for something.'

'This?' Edgar reached over the leather-topped knee-hole desk behind him and picked up a brown, boxlike contraption from the chair where it had been out of sight.

Citrine gasped. 'My Klepteffigium! Give it back!'

Edgar smirked, and before Citrine could stop him he tossed the Klepteffigium into the safe, closed the door and spun the combination lock. 'There. Now you can't take any more nasty Depictions.'

Citrine was fuming. 'What? Have you gone mad? I haven't taken any of you. If Father was here, you wouldn't dare to treat me like this.'

'Perhaps not, but the fact is dear Uncle Hubert's gone, and he can't rule me from the grave.'

'I think he might,' said Citrine, unable to help herself, thinking of Florian's earlier revelation.

Edgar's face went dark as thunder and his hazel eyes glinted dangerously. He picked up a paperknife, the handle decorated with the Capodel crest, and pointed it at her. 'I'm warning you, Citrine,' he said through gritted teeth, 'nanyone will get in my way – not Hubert, not Florian and especially not you.' He pushed her roughly aside and left the room.

'One day I'll find out what really happened,' called Citrine after him. 'Until then, unlike you, I prefer to believe that Father might still be alive.'

She closed the study door, shaking from the intensity of her anger, annoyed with herself for losing her temper and more than a little alarmed at the way Edgar had brandished the paperknife. She stood in front of the safe, hands on hips, but she knew she couldn't possibly open it. Edgar had set a new combination. With the news about the will she had an ominous feeling that things in the Capodel household were going to change, and not for the better. Frustrated, she sat behind the desk, deep in thought. It was almost 12 Nox before she jumped up.

'I shall go to see Florian. He'll tell me what to do.'

Shortly afterwards Citrine's Trikuklos turned on to the street outside the Capodel Townhouse and took off down the steep incline of Collis Hill. She drove across Mercator Square and continued along the cobbled side streets until she reached Malpraxis Mews, where she brought the machine to a skilful halt in the courtyard. She ran over to Florian's green door and grasped the knocker before noticing that the door was already open. Hesitantly she stepped into the warmth of the hall. A white cat hurried towards her and weaved in and out of her legs.

'Hello, Henry,' she whispered, reaching down to scratch

behind his ear. 'Where's Mr Quince? And why is the door open?'

The cat ran off and Citrine went quietly down the hall to Florian's office and poked her head around the door. The lights were low and she could not see very much, but she could smell the familiar aroma of the old legal books that were packed into the shelves on three sides of the room. But tonight there was another, different, odour. Citrine screwed up her nose worriedly. Something was scorching.

Florian was asleep in his wing chair by the dying fire and it was one of his trouser legs that was smouldering. She went over to him and touched him gently on the shoulder. Immediately, with a sharp intake of breath, she recoiled, almost tripping on something underfoot. Florian was dead. Instantly a vision of the third card flashed into her head, the three corvids pulling at the bloody entrails.

'So this is Death,' she whispered.

Shakily she turned up the lights and gasped as she illuminated a scene of confusion. The room was in utter disarray. Papers were scattered across the floor, books teetered half off their shelves and the desk drawers were rifled and hung out of their seats.

'Domna! What in Aether happened here?'

Citrine forced herself to look closely at the aged solicitor. Florian had not died a peaceful death, that much was obvious from the grimace of horror frozen on his face. His eyes were wide, fixed in a horrified stare, the whites bloodshot; his mouth was open in a silent scream. The front of his smoking jacket was stained with blood that had run from a deep wound in his chest.

With shaking hands Citrine closed his eyelids. She spotted a small white fleck between his collar and neck and picked it out; it was a broken fingernail. Florian's nails were short and evenly filed; could it belong to the murderer, broken off in the struggle? The thought disgusted her. She looked closely at the old man's neck. Certainly there were scratches on it, one deep bloodied tear and bruising. Citrine put the nail in her locket, carefully concealing it behind the tiny Depiction of her father. There was little more she could do.

Moments later Citrine was pedalating away. Her mind was working furiously. Was it a coincidence that Florian had died so soon after the row with Edgar? She shook the suspicion from her mind. Edgar might be cruel and selfish, but he was the only family she had left. She looked out for an Urban Guardsman, but where were they when you needed them? Probably all down at the Tar Pit. It wasn't unknown during the festival for some overenthusiastic revellers to get themselves into trouble on the tar-clagged shore. So she headed for home. Much as it galled her, she would have to tell Edgar what had happened.

Back at the Capodel Townhouse, her Trikuklos safely stowed, Citrine looked for her cousin, but he was nowhere to be found. She hurried upstairs; he was not in his room so she went to her own. As soon as she stepped inside she noticed how cold it was. The French windows were wide open.

Did I not close them? she wondered, and then her heart jumped violently in her chest; *there was someone on the balcony.* She looked around frantically for something with which to defend herself. A black pluvitectum was leaning against the wall so she grabbed it. She saw two hands part the flapping curtains and she raised the pluvitectum above her head, ready to fend off the intruder.

'Whoa!' said Edgar, disengaging himself from the curtains. 'What's that for? Expecting rain indoors?'

Citrine lowered the makeshift weapon. 'Domna, you gave me a shock!' she exclaimed. She didn't even bother to ask what he was doing in her room. 'I have to talk to you; something terrible has happened. Florian is dead!'

Edgar closed the French windows very deliberately behind him. Small spots of red began to burn on his cheeks. 'Dead? How do you know?'

'I found him in his office tonight.'

'You've been to his office? But it's the middle of Nox!' Edgar couldn't hide his anger. The muscles in his cheeks were clenching and unclenching.

'I think it was a robbery. It hadn't long happened. Florian was still . . . warm.'

'You need a drink,' said Edgar, suddenly sounding concerned. 'I took the liberty of bringing up a tray. Brandy is good for a shock.'

Citrine saw then the silver tray on the dressing table and the decanter and two cut-crystal tumblers. Edgar turned his back to her and she heard the chink of the stopper. He faced her again and handed her one of the glasses. Aware all the time of his eyes fixed on her, she sipped at the golden liquid. It burned and caused her to cough, but soon it began to warm her insides right down to the bottom of her stomach. She took another, longer, draught. It was sweeter than she had thought it would be.

Edgar appeared to have composed himself somewhat. 'Have you told anyone of this? An Urban Guardsman perhaps?'

'No, but shouldn't we report this now?'

Edgar brought his own glass to his mouth and allowed it to linger on his lips. Unconsciously Citrine mimicked him and took another drink. It was making her feel pleasantly warm inside, and a little light-headed.

'You were wrong to go out so late,' said Edgar. 'And on your own. Degringolade is a dangerous place, especially for a Capodel. Look what happened to your father.'

74

Citrine put her hand to her head. She felt a little nauseous and was finding it difficult to concentrate. Edgar was watching her, his head cocked to one side. He looked amused. Later she remembered thinking that it was an odd expression under the circumstances.

'We don't actually know what happened to Father,' she said with a yawn. 'Shouldn't you be going to get a guardsman?' She yawned again. It was hard to stop.

'Leave it all to me,' continued Edgar easily. But he stayed where he was. He put down his drink and leaned back against the dressing table. He steepled his fingers and somehow they looked different. Citrine knew that it meant something, but she couldn't quite understand what. Now she felt sickeningly dizzy. There was a terrible rushing noise in her head.

'Edgar,' she managed to whisper, 'help me. There's something wrong with me.'

But Edgar was unmoved. He watched as Citrine fell to the floor. And the last things she saw, she saw in great detail: the long white hair on his trouser leg and the ragged nail on the middle finger of his right hand.

CHAPTER 11
A LOSS

Vincent gave one final push at the unyielding trapdoor before sinking to the steps in defeat. Obviously someone had put something heavy on top. He had brought the key as a matter of habit, but there was no way he could push up the trapdoor. He thumped the step in frustration.

'How could I have been so stupid?'

He knew he had acted rashly and he was paying the price. He groaned as the realization of what had really happened dawned on him. Kamptulicon had obviously shut him in. But why hadn't he come down to confront him straight away? That alone was very worrying. And now all he could do was to wait for the ersatz oil vendor to come back and hope he could then somehow escape.

The tunnel was so short and narrow he could not conceal himself there, so he had no choice but to return to the chamber. He had a plan, of sorts; as soon as Kamptulicon appeared, he was going to run at him, knock him to the floor and get the Aether out of there. With this in mind he spent another few minutes looking for a suitable weapon. He had his treen dagger of course, but he hoped to avoid bloodshed. He was a thief but not a violent one. Finally he settled on a short thick baton he found near the humming cabinet.

He took up a position crouched near the chamber entrance, then changed his mind and crept under the table, before finally scooting to the far side of the room and hiding in among a collection of tea chests. Briefly he thought about going into the humming cabinet, but sense prevailed. Apart from the fact that it would have been a squeeze, facing up to Kamptulicon was far preferable to death by freezing.

If he had had the advantage of foresight he might well have changed his mind.

He settled down, alert and armed, truncheon in hand and a dagger on his belt. And so, berating himself all the while – his father would never have been caught in such a trap – he dug in for an uncomfortable wait.

Vincent smelled their arrival before he heard it. A rotten stench rolled down the tunnel and filled the chamber. He had to hold his hand over his nose. Spletivus, what could stink like that? he wondered.

He reached for the gas mask, but to his dismay it was no longer on his belt and there was no time to look for it. He readied himself for the confrontation. He felt the truncheon in his hand, but his palm was sweating. His father had maintained that planning, wit and agility meant there was no need for weapons.

As Kamptulicon's shadow filled the doorway he started to rise, but then he saw that the incomer was not alone. A man, at least he thought it was a man, followed Kamptulicon into the chamber, and he was undoubtedly the source of the smell. Vincent swallowed hard in disbelief. The fellow looked as if he had been dug up from the grave. Then, to compound his horror, Kamptulicon headed straight for the tea chests and smiled.

'Come out, boy, come out! I know you're there! Don't worry, I won't hurt you.'

Vincent knew he had no choice but to show himself. He sheathed his treen dagger, tucked the truncheon under his coat and stood up. 'Mr Kamptulicon, sir,' he began, 'I didn't mean any harm.'

Kamptulicon wasn't one for excuses. Barely had he acknowledged Vincent with a nod of his head than he flicked out the fingers of his right hand. Instantly Vincent felt a burning liquid spatter across his face. Frantically he tried to wipe it away, but when he managed to stop blinking he realized that he couldn't see. Blinded, he was now at Kamptulicon's mercy. His legs were kicked from under him, he crashed to the floor and then there was nothing.

Vincent opened his eyes. Everything was blurred; he could only see shapes, nothing distinct, and it didn't help that there was a bright light shining on his face. He lunged forward but was immediately pulled up sharply and painfully by a strap around his neck. He realized then that he was in the torture chair, held fast by the ankles and wrists. The contents of his pockets had been emptied into a pile on the floor, smitelight and treen included.

The light moved aside, his sight cleared and Kamptulicon came into view. The other man, even uglier close up, stood behind him. Vincent knew he was in grave danger. What would his father do? He appealed again, more humbly, to his captor.

'Mr Kamptulicon, sir, forgive a foolish boy his curiosity. Please, may I go free?'

'Free? Who is there on this earth who can say that he is truly free?' Kamptulicon cocked his head to one side, an insincere smile drawn across his face. 'Now tell me, what is your name?'

'Vincent.'

'Are you alone?'

'Yes,' admitted Vincent reluctantly.

'Good. I need some things from you.' Kamptulicon reached forward and yanked out a handful of Vincent's hair.

'Ouch!' Vincent felt as if his head was on fire.

'Patience,' said Kamptulicon. He dropped the hair into a black stone mortar. Next, with a pair of scissors, he snipped off the fingernails of his prisoner's right hand, practically down to the quick, and Vincent heard them dropping lightly into the mortar. Never had he felt so totally helpless.

'Nearly finished,' said Kamptulicon, and thrust a mortar under Vincent's chin. 'Spit,' he ordered.

Vincent's mouth was dry but he managed a small amount of spittle. 'Is that it?' he asked. 'Have you got what you need?'

'Yes, thank you,' said Kamptulicon with disarming politeness. He put the mortar on the table and spent the next few minutes grinding away at the ingredients. He stopped to add a little water, some green powder and seven drops of cajaput oil (Vincent counted them out), and then continued pounding until it was a smooth waxy paste. He flicked open the top of his large thumb ring and, scooping the paste on to a narrow blade, transferred it into the hollow of the ring. Then he cleaned out the bowl with his finger and smeared the remainder across Vincent's forehead. It stung sharply and Vincent writhed painfully until it subsided.

'What are you doing?' he asked, struggling futilely against his bonds.

'Just a little concoction to help things along,' said

Kamptulicon. 'Now, what is this?' He was holding up the smitelight.

'It's nothing important.' Vincent didn't see the blow coming. It left his head spinning. 'It's a light. Tap it.' Kamptulicon did as was suggested, but on Vincent's head, causing him to see more stars.

'Extraordinary,' he said. 'I haven't seen anything like it. Where did you get it?'

'I don't remember,' muttered Vincent warily.

'Hmm,' mused his captor. He held up Vincent's pouch of treen. 'Gaboon ebony, very nice. The tools of a thief. So, who sent you?'

'No one sent me, I swear. I came of my own accord.'

'You were going to steal from me. I don't like thieves.'

Vincent had a terrible feeling that time was running out. He forced himself to speak calmly despite the gut-wrenching turmoil inside. 'I have caused no damage. Please let me go.'

Kamptulicon ignored his plea. 'I have some tools of my own. Would you like to see them?' He didn't wait for Vincent's reply but reached down and took the metal cylinder from the pile at his feet.

'What's that?' asked Vincent.

'It doesn't have a name yet; it's a recent invention, but it has many uses.'

Something in Kamptulicon's eyes frightened Vincent to

the core. His heart was racing, fuelled by the panic that was rising inside him.

'You see,' said Kamptulicon, slowly unscrewing the lid, 'I think you need to learn a lesson.' A white mist was leaking out from underneath the loosened lid, causing the air around Vincent to cool noticeably. He shuddered. What possible harm could a cold metal cylinder cause?

He was about to find out.

In one coordinated move Kamptulicon removed the lid fully, grabbed Vincent by the right wrist and shoved his hand into the cylinder. For a split second Vincent felt nothing, and then an acute burning pain.

He screamed.

After a few agonizing moments Kamptulicon pulled the cylinder away and replaced the lid. But the pain didn't subside, it worsened.

'What . . . in . . . Aether . . . was . . . that?' Vincent managed to ask in between gasps. The pain was still intensifying, but Kamptulicon had moved on. He put down the cylinder and pulled a pendant on a long chain from around his neck and held it aloft. The putrefying man, who until now had stood motionless, stirred. Kamptulicon cried out,

'*Assumate puer!*'

Vincent now understood the literal meaning of the word 'petrified'. He was for all intents and purposes turned to stone, such was the fear that gripped him. The monstrous man advanced towards him. He was appalling to behold, with his ravaged skin and his masticating mouth and his dull eyes. He looked as if he had succumbed to some terrible wasting disease. Closer and closer he came, and Vincent felt as if his heart was being squeezed to a pulp by a great fist of terror inside his ribs.

The stinking monster leaned forward, and its breath was so cold it burned. Vincent recoiled as far as he could, pressing against the hard upright back of the chair. He tried to turn his head away from the monster, but the strap around his neck started to choke him. He opened his mouth to scream, but no sound came out. And then the dreadful face swooped down to fix its foul lips over Vincent's in a repulsive kiss.

Somehow Vincent knew that it was a kiss of death. The monster's eyes held no pity, just pure evil. He shivered violently. He wanted to close his eyes, to block out the sight, but he was unable. The stench was overwhelming. His stomach was heaving.

I am to die, he thought, alone here in this vile underground chamber, like a rat in a trap, at the hands of two madmen . . .'

At that instant there was a tremendous boom and the room lit up with a dazzling light. Something hard, pellets of some sort, showered down on him, like a thousand pins pricking at his exposed skin. He heard slashing noises and his hands were free, then his feet and head. Someone was trying to drag him from the chair, but he resisted, afraid that it was the monster, until he heard a voice in his ear:

'Run, run! We've got to go!'

A third person, cloaked darkly, was now in the chamber. Vincent stopped struggling and got to his feet. In a second or two he glanced around and saw Kamptulicon lying spreadeagled on the floor. And beside him the monster was kneeling and raking his hands across the flagstones, frenziedly gathering up the black pellets that lay scattered.

'Hurry!' insisted an urgent voice from within the darkness of the hood. Vincent, dazed and confused, just managed to scoop up his treen pouch before allowing himself to be led away past Kamptulicon's inert body and along the tunnel, up the stairs and finally outside into the cool night air.

CHAPTER 12
BETRAYED!

When Citrine opened her eyes, she was immediately aware of two things. One, she was in a very dark place and, two, she was lying on her back on a hard bed that was most certainly not hers. Her head was pounding and she was finding it difficult to gather her thoughts.

She sat up and leaned against the nearest wall. Its cold dampness penetrated her clothes.

Where in Aether's name am I? she wondered, for this was no room in the Capodel Townhouse. 'And what *is* that smell?' It was a mixture of musty fungus and other nasty aromas she preferred not to identify. A drop of water splashed on to her hand. She looked up. Above her head there was a barred window. Cautiously she stood on the bed. She was just tall enough to see the grey buildings outside, and behind them the unmistakable silhouette of the Kronometer against the night sky. It was comforting to know that she was still in Degringolade. But where was she? How long had she been asleep?

On the floor beside the bed was a newspaper, the *Degringolade Daily*. She squinted to read it in the poor light. According to the date she had been here at least a day. The headline was like a punch in the stomach.

Young Heiress Brutally Murders Family Solicitor for Money
More Mystery and Tragedy for the Capodel Family
Reported by Hepatic Whitlock

Citrine Capodel, daughter of missing businessman Hubert Capodel, has been charged with the murder of local solicitor Florian Quince. Evidence at the scene of Mr Quince's murder points undeniably to young Miss Capodel's guilt. Chief Guardsman Mayhew Fessup made the following statement:

'The use of Digital Dermal Configuration Diagnosis has established that it was indeed Citrine's very own hand of evil that wielded the Fatal Knife that brought about the death of Mr Quince. Her DermaCons were found clear as day in the blood on the handle of the murder weapon.'

For the more scientifically minded readers among you, 'Digital Dermal Configuration Diagnosis' is a method whereby the unique patterns made by a person's fingertips – or DermaCons, as they are known – found at the scene of a crime

86

are set in ink and compared to the patterns on the fingertips of the suspect. If the two match then guilt is proven beyond doubt. Scientists believe that no two sets of DermaCons are the same (though some maintain that identical twins might be a possible exception).

Governor d'Avidus praised CG Fessup for the speed with which Citrine Capodel was arrested. 'Good investigation is a mixture of science and gut feeling,' said Mr d'Avidus, 'and Mayhew Fessup employs both liberally.'

Of course, this all begs the question, just what would drive a young heiress to such extraordinary lengths . . . ?

Aghast, Citrine read the article a second time, hardly able to take in what it was saying. Her DermaCons found on the murder weapon? She examined her fingertips, looking closely at the whorls and the lines and arcs. They were stained black, from the ink, she realized, but what was that under her nails? Was it blood?

Worriedly, Citrine crossed the small room to the door. It was metal, grey and cool to the touch, with round-headed rivets running up and down its surface. At eye level there was a small flap that dropped down to form a shelf on her side of the door. The hole it left was covered by sliding grille on the outer side. It wasn't fully closed and Citrine managed to poke her index finger into the gap and push it to one side.

She looked out on to an empty, gloomy corridor. Candles sputtered along the walls. She could see more doors, the same as hers, opposite and up and down the corridor, but it was only when she heard the cursing and swearing and shouting from behind them that she understood the true nature of her situation.

'Domna, Edgar!' she exclaimed. 'What have you done to me?'

Citrine was in the Degringolade Penitentiary.

Chapter 13
Triskaidekaphobia
Author's Note

'Triskaidekaphobia' is the fear of the number thirteen. Degringoladians, being so superstitious, always consider it an unlucky number. So, in keeping with Degringoladian tradition, there is no chapter thirteen in this book.

Chapter 14

Rabbit Stew

Vincent lifted his head. His stirring brain was flooded with a confusion of memories: the chair, Leopold Kamptulicon's grinning face, the stench of the monster . . .

'Good, you're awake at last,' said a voice close by.

His vision cleared and the figure kneeling beside him came into focus. He saw a shock of cropped blonde hair, so blonde it was almost white, and eyes of the darkest blue.

'Oh,' said Vincent. 'You're a girl.'

'My name is Folly Harpelaine. Who are you?'

'I'm Vincent.' He struggled into a sitting position. His right arm didn't seem to be working properly, and when he looked at it he saw that it was bandaged. 'How long have I been asleep?'

'A night and a day. It's night again. Here.' Folly held out a tin cup. 'Drink. Antikamnial, for the pain.'

Cautiously Vincent sipped the cloudy water. The steamy aroma seemed to clear his head. He held up his bandaged arm; it was like a lead weight. He regarded it quizzically. 'What happened?'

'Don't you remember what Kamptulicon did to you?'

Vincent thought hard. 'He had some sort of icy metal cylinder. Spletivus, but it was cold! And it burned.'

'I think he froze your hand.'

Vincent managed a laugh. 'Froze my hand? Is that all?' He took his arm out of the sling and examined the bandages.

'Well, it could have been worse. You still have your thumb and forefinger.'

Vincent looked up sharply. 'What are you talking about?'

'I'm sorry, Vincent,' said Folly matter-of-factly. 'There was nothing I could do. Whatever that cylinder was, it froze your hand so badly that three of your fingers practically broke off. You must have had your thumb and forefinger tucked under – that's the only reason I can think they survived.'

Vincent's already white face paled further. 'I've lost three fingers on my right hand? No!' Frenziedly he began to rip at the bandages, desperate to know the truth, ignoring the pain.

'Stop,' said Folly sternly. 'Let me do it. Your hand needs to heal. You don't want to lose what's left as well, do you?'

Vincent let his good arm drop to the blanket and held his right hand to his chest. He could feel his heart pounding. He gestured to the bandages. 'Did you do this?'

'Yes, and I stitched up your hand. I gave you Antikamnial

to dull the pain and a cordial to help you to sleep. Now it's time to change the bandages again.'

Wordlessly, Vincent watched in trepidation as Folly unwound the stained length of material. The wound itself was covered in gauze, discoloured by the fluid that seeped from the injured flesh. Unfortunately it was stuck to the skin and Vincent shouted out as she peeled it away.

'Spletivus, take it easy!'

'Sorry. Don't turn away – you'll have to get used to it. It's not so bad.'

Vincent steeled himself, took a deep breath and stared down.

The knuckles were swollen and red, and where his fingers should have been there was a blunt rawness and dried black blood. Folly had done as good a job as any master surgeon, her stitches were even and small, but it was still a shocking sight. 'That's . . . disgusting,' he whispered. He felt physically sick at the sight.

Folly was dabbing carefully at the stitches, wiping the skin with a piece of cloth soaked in the warm salted water. It stung and Vincent feared he was going to cry.

'You're lucky,' said Folly brightly as she reached for a small terracotta pot at her side. 'It's not infected. I'll bandage it up again, but not quite so thickly.'

She unscrewed the lid and dipped her second and third

finger into the yellow unguent within, then smeared it across the stunted end of his hand. Immediately the stinging sensation subsided and Vincent felt warmth spreading over the damaged skin.

'Thank you,' he mumbled, swallowing hard. A tear squeezed out of the corner of his eye, but he thought she had not noticed. He sniffed and took a deep breath, then forced himself to look again at the bloody mutilation that was his right hand. 'I suppose I should be glad I'm left-handed,' he said.

'You should get up now,' said Folly, standing herself. 'You need to move around. You've been lying there for long enough. I'm making slumgullion. You look like you could do with a good meal. And after that perhaps you can explain what business you have with Leopold Kamptulicon.'

Vincent allowed Folly to help him across the room to what served as a table, a large block of off-white marble shot through with spidery veins of black. While Folly stirred the pot that hung over the fire, he took the opportunity to examine his surroundings. The stone-walled room was windowless, the only way out through a wide, heavy-looking door at the top of ten steps. There was a black leather coat hanging on one wall, a gas mask beside it, and in another corner there was a small trunk.

He had only a hazy recollection of the journey here; racing

along city streets, trudging across a dark marsh – he thought he remembered statues but he couldn't be sure.

'Slumgullion's up.'

Folly was setting the pot on the table, wielding, rather than holding, a ladle. 'It's rabbit,' she said. 'I caught a couple yesterday. The Komaterion's overrun with them – must be the quality of the grass.'

Komaterion? Vincent looked around and saw the niches in the walls, the fat urns and the stone casket opposite. 'This is a burial chamber?' he blurted out.

'They call it a Kryptos in these parts,' said Folly.

'But it has a fireplace!'

'Traditional in Degringolade. Kryptoi are all equipped with fireplaces in case the owner comes back from the dead. Years ago someone used to wait with the body for a week, to make sure they were dead, and they needed a fire to keep warm.'

'Oh,' was all he could think of to say.

Folly handed him a bowl of what looked like lumpy soup. Vincent would have demurred but for the gnawing hunger in his guts. He was pleased to discover that what this slumgullion lacked in appearance it made up for in taste. Folly filled both their cups with a herbal tisane.

They ate in silence. As the slumgullion warmed him through, Vincent began to feel better. He took a drink of the tisane and washed it around the inside of his mouth. It tasted of quince and fennel, and something else he couldn't identify. He smiled wryly to himself; although he had been in many strange places and situations in his life, this was the first time he had eaten in what was essentially a grave.

But if physically he felt more at ease, his mind was far from carefree. He finished his stew, steadying the bowl carefully against his right arm so as to be able to scrape every last drop from the sides.

'Thank you, Folly,' he said suddenly, almost as an afterthought, 'for saving me from that madman Kamptulicon.' He did not make a habit of thanking people; he prided himself on rarely being in debt to anyone, especially for his life. His father had taught him that. Folly merely nodded, still eating, so he went for a closer look at the casket. He brushed away the sticky cobwebs to reveal a plaque on the side and read the copperplate inscription:

Lady Scarletta Degringolade –
Requiescas in Pace, Domna

'So the city of Degringolade takes its name from a family?'

Folly nodded. 'A brutal lot. They spent centuries fighting amongst themselves over land and money. There's more than a few met their end in the Tar Pit. They're all dead now, and

Degringolade Manor is dilapidated. And it's all salt marsh round here, from when the sea flooded the land.' Folly's face changed and took on a serious aspect. Vincent had a feeling he knew what she was going to say.

'So, anyway, how did you end up in Kamptulicon's . . . ahem . . . special chair?'

'I was . . . er . . . looking for something.'

Folly regarded him coolly and shrugged. 'I understand. Did he take anything from you?'

'My fingers,' said Vincent bitterly. 'And hair and spit and nails.' He touched his forehead where Kamptulicon had smeared the paste. The skin was red and blistered. 'And my smitelight. But I'll get it back, whatever it takes, and they'll pay, him and his stinking friend, for what they've done to me.'

Folly gave him an odd smile. 'I don't think you understand what you're dealing with, Vincent. Kamptulicon's "stinking friend" is a Lurid. You know, one of the Supermundane entities.' She stated this as if expecting him to know what she was talking about.

'Super-what?'

'A true Vulgar,' she murmured.

'What did you say?'

'Not from round here,' said Folly without missing a beat. 'Supermundane refers to all matters outside what we might consider normalcy; events that cannot be explained, entities that can or cannot be seen. Lurids are just one such creature.'

Vincent shook his head. 'I was told that Lurids are trapped by salt.'

Folly frowned. 'Normally they are, but Kamptulicon has set one free. I saw him do it. Domne, but I wish I knew how. We need to watch ourselves now or—'

'Forget "we",' said Vincent firmly. 'There's no "we" in this. I work alone.' Folly shot him a look and, fearing that he had upset her, Vincent flashed his smile. 'I don't mean to sound ungrateful, but this is between me and that maggot Kamptulicon.'

Folly's face remained impenetrable. 'Surely you value your life more than, what did you call it, a smitelight?'

'My father gave me that smitelight before he died. I want it back.'

'I'm sorry,' said Folly. 'My father is dead too.'

'He was the best picklock there ever was,' said Vincent proudly.

'What happened?'

'He was killed by a rival. That's why I want my smitelight back. It's all I have to remember him by.'

'And what will you do if you get it?'

'If? You mean when! I'll move on, of course. I don't like to stay in the same place for too long. And Degringolade is not quite what I was expecting.'

'Antithica province is not quite like anywhere else,' stressed Folly, and began to clear away the table. 'I'll give you directions back to Degringolade, if you're sure that's what you want, but it's not easy to cross the salt marsh in the dark; it can play tricks on you.'

'I'll manage,' said Vincent. He had been in far more dangerous places than a marsh. He wasn't going to let this rather odd girl put him off.

'Of course, I'm not sure how you'll fare when Kamptulicon and his Lurid come after you,' continued Folly casually. 'I mean, you didn't do so well last time.'

Vincent looked at his bandaged hand and suddenly he wasn't quite so confident any more. A wave of exhaustion rolled over him and he sat back down. He felt weak and, something else he wasn't used to, out of control. He knew he had to stay on top of things, not make reckless decisions. His father's advice rang in his ears: *Don't cut off your nose to spite your face. Sometimes you have to accept things as they are.*

'I just thought you might appreciate some help from someone who knows a little more about these things than you do,' Folly was saying. 'And who has two working hands. But, if you think you can do it alone . . .'

'OK, maybe you're right,' he conceded wearily. 'I don't feel too good.'

'You don't look too good. You need more Antikamnial and rest. You'll be safe here. Lurids can't come into the Komaterion. Hallowed ground, you see.'

Vincent didn't see, but he hadn't the energy to argue. 'Just for tonight then,' he agreed. 'But I haven't changed my mind.' He went slowly to his mattress and lay down. He felt like a deflated pig's bladder. 'Lurids! It's all just superstitious nonsense,' he murmured as his eyes closed. 'Hey, Folly, answer me this – why were you at Kamptulicon's?'

He was asleep before Folly could answer. She watched him for a short while, until the rhythm of his breathing settled, and then sat by the fire and opened the little book she had taken from his boot heel. A frown of concentration etched across her forehead, she began to read.

CHAPTER 15
A LIKELY STORY

Citrine sat on the bed and stared at the ragged piece of fingernail that lay in her palm, Edgar's fingernail. 'There must be another explanation for this,' she kept telling herself. But there wasn't. It was patently clear to her now; Edgar had killed Florian with the paperknife he had taken from Hubert's study. Then he had come back to the house and waited for her. He had drugged her drink and put the bloodied knife in her hand to get her DermaCons. 'And he must have paid someone in the DUG to make sure I was taken to the penitentiary,' she concluded. She took a deep breath. If she was right, she knew she could no longer ignore her other suspicion: the possibility that Edgar was in some way responsible for the disappearance of her father.

Startled by the rattle of a key in the lock, Citrine jumped up as the cell door swung open.

'Oh, it's you,' she said coldly as Edgar came into the cell. There were two other people with him: a jailer, a large fellow in a grey ill-fitting uniform who hovered at the door and a stern-faced man, smartly dressed in the frock coat and bowler hat of a senior member of the DUG.

'Dear cousin,' said Edgar, as if greeting Citrine in the comfort of her drawing room, 'I trust you are happy with your accommodation. I thought you would prefer to be on your own rather than to share with the scum of the streets of Degringolade. This fellow here is Chief Guardsman Mayhew Fessup of the DUG. He would like to ask you some questions.'

The two men almost filled the small space and Citrine was forced backwards until her legs bumped against the bed.

Fessup cleared his throat and spoke sternly. 'You should be very grateful to your cousin. I can imagine that penitentiary life must be really quite shocking to you, but with crime comes consequence. You could hardly have expected to get away with it.'

'Get away with what?' asked Citrine hotly. 'Do you mean this nonsense?' She held up the *Degringolade Daily*.

Fessup tutted. 'All this denial will not save you from the gallows.'

Citrine's mouth fell open. 'The gallows?'

'Well, that's where you're going. Unless you can explain how the bloodstained paperknife with the Capodel crest on it that killed Florian Quince was found under your mattress. Your DermaCons were clear as day on the handle.'

Citrine felt her eyes stretch to their limit. 'But Florian

101

was already dead when I found him!'

Edgar exchanged a knowing glance with Fessup, as if to say, 'I told you so.'

Citrine grabbed at Fessup's sleeve. 'You cannot believe that I would do this,' she insisted. 'Florian Quince was a great friend of my dear father and my friend too. Why would I kill him?'

Fessup shrugged her off. 'In my experience people kill for one of three reasons: romantic love, money and out of lunacy. Did you love Mr Quince?'

'No,' said Citrine with great indignation.

'Are you mad?'

'I'm as sane as you are!'

'Then you must have done it for money,' concluded Fessup with obvious satisfaction.

'Money?' Citrine could not believe her ears. 'I have no need for money. I'm Citrine Capodel!'

'We found the will in your room,' said Edgar. 'The one you stole from Florian's study. You killed Florian, the only living witness to the original will, and forged a new one in your favour.'

Citrine couldn't speak, rendered momentarily dumb with shock.

'Jealousy is a terrible thing,' said Edgar sorrowfully. 'When you found out I was to inherit everything, well—'

'You filthy liar!' screeched Citrine, and she began to rain down blows on Edgar's chest.

Edgar pushed her away. 'Take your bloodstained hands off me,' he said harshly, and strode out of the cell.

'It's up to the judge now,' said Fessup, and he tipped his hat and left. The door closed with an ill-boding clang and the key turned in the lock with devastating finality.

'Yes, put me before the judge,' shouted Citrine through the grille, 'and see how your lies stand up in court.'

She turned and leaned her back against the door. This couldn't be happening to her, a Capodel! Her world had been turned upside down twice in under a year, but this time her very life was in danger. She had to do something, but what? She paced restlessly for hours, her mind racing, before finally lying on the lumpy bed and drifting off into a disturbed sleep.

She woke to the sound of the grille sliding back. There was a tray on the shelf. 'Something to keep you going, Miss Citrine,' called a gruff voice.

Taken aback at the unexpected kindness, Citrine roused herself and went to the door. The jailer from earlier was standing outside. He cast a broad shadow on the wall, such was the width of his shoulders, and the collar of his grey uniform sat high about his ears. His dark hair was long with a slight wave, and he held his head in such a way as to cause it to fall over his eyes. Something glinted from under his hair when he moved his head, a gold earring with a protective green zircon stone in the centre.

'Kew,' she said quietly. 'Do you happen to know what hour it is?'

'Just after two bells, miss.'

'Two bells?'

'Oh, sorry, Miss Citrine, old habits die hard. It's early Lux. I used to work on a whaling ship, see. I was the youngest feller on board, but I was a crack shot with a whale spear.'

Citrine could hear both pride and regret in his voice, and something else, something familiar. 'What's your name?'

'Jonah Scrimshander.'

Citrine made a small exclamation. 'Jonah! The fellow I ran over with my Trikuklos!'

She heard a sharp intake of breath and Jonah came a little closer. 'That was you? But the *Degringolade Daily* says you murdered someone.'

'You don't believe that, do you?'

There was a short pause before Jonah answered. 'Lookin' at you, and hearin' you, I find it hard to believe that you would do such a thing. You gave me a sequentury. Not many rich folk'd do that. There's people in this city would have run me over a second time for sport.'

'Jonah, believe me, it's all a terrible mistake. They are talking about sending me to the gallows!'

'They string 'em up for a lot less,' he said grimly, and not at all helpfully.

'But, Jonah, I am innocent! I would pay you whatever you asked if you got me out of this wretched place.' Now she wished again that she had given him more than a sequentury.

Jonah laughed. 'Everyone's innocent in here. Aether knows I hates to see injustice, if that's what this is, but I have to think of meself. If I help you, it would be the end for me if anyone found out. I have no other way to earn a living. Nanyone wants to see the likes of me out on the street.'

He came forward and removed his hat, pushed back his hair and turned down his collar. He held up his manuslantern and for the first time showed Citrine his face. She stifled a gasp and recoiled involuntarily. Jonah was dreadfully scarred; long, red, raised weals stretched the full length of each cheek. And on the backs of his hands similar scars caused his callused fingers to claw.

Citrine saw his look of distress. 'I'm sorry,' she said quickly. 'I didn't expect . . .'

'It's all right.' He retreated, raising his collar again. 'Now you see why I prefer to work in a place like this, out of sight of normal folk.'

'What happened to you? Were you in a fire or a chemical accident?'

'If you must know, Miss Citrine, I was swallered by a Cachelot.'

Citrine looked bemused. 'Swallered . . . swallowed, by a Cachelot?'

'A sort of whale, the largest creature in the ocean, but rare as turkey teeth. There's barely a sailor alive who can claim to have seen one in his lifetime. And the day I saw a Cachelot is a day that has been etched into my very skin. I thought my eyes were lyin' to me. It was of enormous proportions. Its flukes alone were almost the length of the ship. Fifty spears I buried in its hide, but still its aquatic gyrations were causing huge waves that threatened at any moment to sink us. As I watched, it looked me straight in the eye and instantly I felt its distress and I was ashamed. What right had I, a mere dwarf beside this monster, to wrest it from its briny home? In that singular moment I knew I could not kill one of Nature's creatures ever again.

'But then the Cachelot's thrashing fluke hit the side of the ship with such force that I was flung overboard and down towards the boiling sea. I braced myself for the cold water but I landed on what could have been firm ground. "By the barnacles," I cried, "I am in the behemoth's mouth!"'

Citrine's eyes widened. 'No! It cannot be true!'

'By a hundred whale's teeth it is,' said Jonah, warming to his subject, and he crossed his heart with his gnarled hand.

'And before I could right myself I was sucked down the creature's throat into a dark cavern of foul-smelling slime. A searing heat spread over my skin; 'twas the liquid poison in its belly that was burning my flesh.'

'So your scars are from the digestive juices of a Cachelot?' exclaimed Citrine.

Jonah nodded. 'That they are, and by Poseidon the beast was in a rage, lurching from side to side, trying to rid itself of the spears. It was dark as Nox in there, and the air, what little there was, was rancid. My lungs were fit to burst. I knew I had only a brief time to escape.'

'But what in Aether could you possibly do?' asked Citrine.

'There's an old whaling saying:

"In the belly of the whale, this trick won't fail, Tickle its tum and up you'll come."

'And that is what I did. I began to rake the walls of this living prison with my hands, over and over, until there was one powerful lurch and I was expelled violently from its mouth back into the sea. I was half dead on the waves, but thank St Nicholas and St Peter, the feller in the crow's nest spotted me. I was hauled aboard. They thought I would die, for I looked like a creature returned from the grave, and still do, but I survived. But I am no longer welcome on board a whaler, nor any ship for that matter, for I am considered unlucky. But in truth I have no wish to harvest the sea's bounty again.' He let out a wry laugh. 'So, what do you say? Am I the luckiest fellow alive or the unluckiest?'

'Oh, the luckiest, beyond all doubt!' exclaimed Citrine. 'Would that I could have some of your luck when I stand before the judge!' She clenched her fists. 'How long must I wait to have my chance to speak the truth?'

Jonah looked doubtful and Citrine thought he was about to say something, but then they both heard footsteps. 'It's Mr Capodel again,' said Jonah, looking down the corridor. 'And there's someone with him.'

When Jonah opened the door Citrine saw Edgar and a stranger, a man. She guessed from the way he beheld her, with detached curiosity, that he was a physician of some sort. He smiled benignly.

'Hello, Citrine. I am Dr Ruislip. I have come to assess you. How are you?'

'How do you think? Look at where I am.'

'Showing aggression and sarcastic humours . . .' murmured Dr Ruislip, and wrote in his notebook.

'All I wish is to be free,' said Citrine, 'and to clear my name.'

'Still in denial,' murmured the doctor, scribbling away.

Edgar spoke. 'Dr Ruislip tells me that if you accept that you are mad, then you will not be hanged, merely incarcerated in the lunatic asylum, where you will undergo suitable treatment to subdue your violent tendencies. If you make sufficient progress, you will be freed, in perhaps ten years or so.'

'Ten years! Never!' shouted Citrine.

Edgar actually looked upset. 'Citrine, for pity's sake, do you think I want to watch you swing?'

'Oh, spare me your crocodile tears,' hissed Citrine. 'It is you should be swinging, you . . . you Janus-faced liar.'

'Come along, Mr Capodel, 'said Dr Ruislip. 'Your cousin is clearly beyond help. Perhaps the hangman's halter is the kindest thing after all.'

Jonah opened the door to allow the men to leave, and Edgar grimaced. 'By God,' he said loudly, 'you're so ugly you should be in travelling show! At least you won't need a costume for the festival.' He walked away laughing loudly at his own joke.

Citrine looked imploringly at Jonah. 'Will you at least consider what I asked? I have proof.'

Jonah raised an eyebrow.

'It's not much, just a fingernail, but it proves that Edgar was at Florian's office.'

Jonah sucked his teeth. 'Let me think on things, Miss Citrine. Eat up your food, such as it is, worser 'n ship's biscuit. I promise I'll be back later.'

'I'll still be here,' said Citrine in a very small voice. 'I hope.'

Chapter 16
On the Trail

Leopold Kamptulicon raised his arms and brought his fists down on the table in incandescent rage. He swept one arm across the surface, scattering its miscellaneous contents. Shards of glass and broken pottery flew around the room.

'The filthy little wretch! He's stolen my book!' He paced up and down the length of the table, debris crunching underfoot, remonstrating with himself. 'And curses on his rescuer! Only seconds more and the Lurid would have assumed his body. Now I have nanything to show for all my effort.'

Kamptulicon gritted his teeth. It physically pained him to remember how his moment of glory had been wrenched so violently from his grasp. The force of the explosion had knocked him right off his feet and he still had a ringing in his ears. 'And it's no ordinary person who rescued him,' he bemoaned, kicking at black pellets with the pointed toe of his shoe. 'This is most definitely not the work of a Vulgar.'

It was imperative that he get the book back. But he would have to tread carefully. Considering what the boy and his blonde accomplice had done here, the chances were they would recognize the book for what it was and know its power. A little calmer now, he went over to the cabinet against the wall and, holding up the pendant with one hand, opened the door with the other.

'*Amok!*' he commanded.

The door opened with a hiss and the Lurid slunk out, its face contorting into one grotesque expression after another. Its smell was not as strong as before, but to Kamptulicon it was not a repulsive odour and he could breathe it in with impunity. He walked around the strange manifestation, observing it from every angle. It was like a three-dimensional shadow of a man. The Lurid's dead eyes fixed on him and it opened its mouth to emit a strangely strangled sound. Kamptulicon covered his ears. 'Domne, wretched creature, desist from that caterwauling!'

He put his hand out and touched it and it was so cold it burned. It was still tangibly solid, but time was not on his side. If he was to deliver what he had promised, then he had to find that boy. A sly smile crossed his face. Surely he deserved some credit for getting this far? To have deciphered the book, and summoned a Lurid and kept it under his control was a hugely impressive achievement in itself. He was so close to his goal he was not going to let anything stop him now. And foresight had given them the means.

Kamptulicon flipped open his thumb ring and held it out to the Lurid. The green paste, the essence of Vincent, glistened within. '*Queste,*' he ordered.

Wordlessly the gurning ghoul performed something approximating a sniffing action. Then, like a dog on the trail of a scent, it crossed the debris-strewn floor to the door and slipped right through it. Kamptulicon, being merely human, exited the room in a more conventional manner and followed the Lurid quickly up the tunnel to the stairs.

Chapter 17
The Lantern Bearers

'Folly?'

Vincent's voice echoed around the Kryptos and a cursory glance told him that he was alone. He threw off the blanket and stretched, and proceeded to make himself a weak tisane from a used bag and eat a piece of bread he found on the table. Then he explored the Kryptos thoroughly. There was little to see: Folly's bedroll, his own makeshift bed, some crockery. He went to the trunk and in a matter of seconds he had sprung the lock and lifted the lid. There were clothes on top – trousers and shirts – and he helped himself to one of each. He also found a compass and a roll of maps, including one of Antithica province and a smaller detailed map of Degringolade. He spread the latter on the table and took a few moments to peruse it. The Flumen River was clearly marked in blue, skirting the city before flowing out to the Turbid Sea.

With his left index finger he traced a path out of Degringolade along the Great West Road to a wide area marked Palus Salus – the salt marsh, he guessed – in the middle of which was the symbol for a Komaterion. Further across, a dark patch indicated the Tar Pit. Folly was making it out to be harder than it was, he thought; all he had to do was follow the path across the marsh and it would lead him back to the city. In a decisive mood, refreshed from sleep and frustrated at having wasted so much time already, he quickly packed up his belongings, including the map and compass, and took a spare manuslantern. 'Goodbye, Folly, whoever you are,' he murmured on the threshold of the Kryptos. 'And thanks for everything.'

He stepped out into semi-darkness and a thick swirling mist. The warm Kryptos suddenly seemed very inviting, but the sight of his bandaged hand steeled his resolve. He set off, whistling to keep himself cheerful, and spent a few hundred yards relishing thoughts of how he might exact his revenge on Kamptulicon, each more grisly than the last. Suddenly he remembered the heel of his boot and stopped to check it. He was not surprised to find that the book was gone. Kamptulicon must have taken that too. Oh, how he would have loved to give the sadistic maggot a taste of his own medicine.

But, if he was completely honest with himself, Vincent knew that all he really wanted was to retrieve his smitelight and go on his way. He was a thief and a picklock with a badly injured hand; Kamptulicon was quite obviously a lunatic with an equally mad and stinking friend. At least *he* couldn't sneak up on him; his smell would always give him away! Yes, he would exact his revenge, but he could wait.

He was heartened, however, by the thought of the mansions on the hill. He would pay one or two a visit before he left Degringolade. He remembered too the green-eyed girl's Trikuklos. What a fine prize that would be. And then he would get the Aether out of this place.

Resolutely he strode on, but the path was increasingly difficult to negotiate, and it wasn't long before he was beginning to feel uneasy. Surely he should be able to see the city lights by now. Once the edge of the path gave way and he sank ankle deep into the marshy verge. 'This'll do my boots no good at all!' he lamented as he pulled his feet out of the sucking mud – they were a particularly fine pair he had stolen prior to his arrival in Degringolade. Back on firmer ground, he checked the compass but the needle was spinning wildly, refusing to settle. His heart sank. How long had he been going the wrong way? To compound his unease, the ever-present howling was increasing in volume and to Vincent, alone out on the dark, inhospitable marsh, the noise seemed rather more menacing than when he had first heard it from his perch in the Kronometer. So, when a cluster of blue lights appeared up ahead in the mist, he hailed the mysterious lantern bearers with some relief.

'Hey!' he shouted. 'Where are you going?' They must have heard for the lights steadied in one place, though no one replied. 'Should I follow?' he wondered. The lights moved on and he found the decision was made for him. 'Wait for me!'

He stumbled towards the lights, but they were always ahead of him. When he slowed, they slowed, and when he speeded up, so too did the lights. 'They're teasing me,' he laughed suddenly. He felt quite light-headed. The tarry smell that had accosted his nose and throat ever since he had arrived in Degringolade was stronger here. He lunged for a light that danced just feet away, lost his footing and began to half roll, half slide downhill, coming to an abrupt and painful halt against some sort of rock. Winded, he lay for a moment before turning on to his stomach and reaching for his manuslantern, which was lying nearby. But when he held it up his stomach twisted with terror. He was lying not on rough gravel, but on a shingle of blackened bones. *Human bones*.

Panicking and desperate to get away from the smell and the agonized wailing, Vincent scrambled to his feet. Racked by a fit of coughing he began gasping for air. But no matter how hard he tried, he couldn't fill his lungs. Then a gap opened up in the mist and instantly he knew where he had come. He was nowhere near Degringolade; he was on the shore of the Tar

Pit. And there, out on its dark bubbling surface, he saw the source of the howling, the horde of swaying Lurids that bayed ceaselessly at the diminishing moon. A sob of fear caught in his throat. There were hundreds of them!

The Lurids sensed his presence and raced towards the shore. Vincent staggered backwards, his limbs heavy and difficult to move, the sticky tar pulling at his boots, and his disbelieving eyes were mesmerized by the ululating mob. His head was spinning, his lungs were contracting and his own moans of terror mingled with those of the advancing Lurids. In an instant of clarity he remembered his gas mask. But it was too late. If he could just get up the slope, away from the noxious lake. But now he was surrounded by tall shapes. People? No, pillars of some sort. He stumbled on, straight into the path of a dark shadow with huge eyes and a long snout. A Degringoladian devil!

Vincent tried to call out, but his voice failed him. He could only croak as he sank to his knees on the sharp bones. The devil creature leaned down and he could see the abject terror on his own face reflected in its glassy eyes. He could hear its heavy breathing, like frothing water. He tried to lift his arms to defend himself, but they wouldn't work.

'Stop fighting me, you fool,' said a muffled voice, 'and put on your mask.'

*

117

Vincent stood in front of the Kryptos fire warming his hands. His lungs still burned slightly when he inhaled but gradually his breathing was improving. Another dose of Antikamnial had taken the edge off his throbbing hand, but nothing could take away the crippling feeling of foolishness.

'You're lucky I came looking for you,' said Folly lightly. 'You wouldn't have lasted much longer. Did you not think to put on your gas mask? And even luckier you could still walk. I couldn't have dragged you back here.'

'I was doing OK until the compass stopped working,' he said defensively.

'Compasses don't work near the Tar Pit. The whole place is full of impedimentium, a magnetic ore; it affects the needle.'

'If it hadn't been for those blue lanterns then.'

'Corpse candles, they're called. The Puca spirits carry them to lead you astray, just for the fun of it. You should never follow them.'

'Puca?' began Vincent, but when he saw the expression on Folly's face he didn't dare to challenge her. Besides, he really wasn't so sure of himself right now. Maybe there was something to all this superstition after all.

Folly continued coolly. 'Anyway, I have something for you.' She held out a tangled mass of metal and leather.

'A present?' Vincent was noticeably taken aback, but his initial look of confusion was quickly replaced by one of

118

recognition and he managed a laugh. 'The artificial arm from the Caveat Emptorium.'

'I saw it and thought of you,' said Folly with the hint of a smile. 'It might make things a little easier. I'll help you put it on.'

Vincent forgot his irritation and pushed up his sleeve. Carefully he placed his mutilated arm into the conical metal shape and down into the glove-like hand. His surviving fingers fitted easily into the thumb and forefinger and he decided not to detach them for the time being. Folly helped him with the web of straps and buckles. 'It might take a bit of getting used to. Wenceslas said that it had some special tricks.'

Vincent turned the hand this way and that. It was surprisingly light and flexible. The surface was rusty and dull, though nothing a good polish wouldn't improve, and the joints creaked a little, but the leather straps were soft and worn. There were three inset sliding switches and a small dial on the underside of the wrist. He pushed one of the switches forward but nothing happened.

'This is marvellous,' he said with a grin. 'I'll be able to hold things again.' He reached for a knife on the table, but before he was near enough to grasp it, the knife slid rapidly towards him and attached itself to one of the metal fingers. 'It's magnetic! I think it was that switch.' Vincent slid the switch back to its original position and instantly the knife clattered to the ground. 'Spletivus! This could be better than a real hand!'

He looked over at Folly, his eyes shining. This was the best he had felt since it had all happened. 'Thanks for saving me, again,' he said. 'You know, to be honest, after what I saw out there on the Tar Pit, I'm starting to believe you . . . about the Lurids.'

Folly laughed. 'Starting? Better late than never, I suppose.'

'It could have been the gases, you know, making me see things,' he retorted. Then he softened his tone and smiled. 'I've been thinking, maybe we can help each other.'

'We? I thought there was no "we".'

'Yes, I know what I said earlier. I wasn't thinking straight – all those potions you gave me. But if you help me to get my smitelight back I'll help you.'

Folly seemed to find the offer amusing. 'But you don't know what I want to do.'

'Nothing I can't handle, I'm sure,' said Vincent chirpily, feeling a little more like his old self.

'It's in your interest, actually. I have to send the Lurid back to the Tar Pit.'

Vincent couldn't help but look surprised. 'Have to? Who says? And, anyway, how is what you do to that stinker in my interest?'

'Because that "stinker" is coming after you.'

Vincent laughed, still flexing his metal hand. 'You're joking.'

But Folly was deadly serious. 'Listen. Kamptulicon has taken advantage of the lunar apogee to free a Lurid. That paste he made binds you to the Lurid, and he wants it to take over your body.'

Vincent grimaced, recalling the Lurid's cold kiss. 'What sort of maniac is this Kamptulicon? Why does he want a Lurid?'

Folly made a gesture of incomprehension with her hands. 'Nany honourable reason, you can be sure,' she said grimly. 'But, as for dealing with the Lurid, I might just have something to help us.' There was an unmistakable twinkle in her eye as she dug into her pocket and pulled out a small black book.

Vincent's mouth fell open.

'A fair swap for my compass and map, don't you think?' Folly grinned. 'I found it when you were asleep. Presumably it's Kamptulicon's, and one more reason he'll be looking for you.'

'It's only a book,' said Vincent rather pettily. He was annoyed, and not just because he had been robbed. He was beginning to think that in Folly he might have met his match.

'A book that could be very useful for us, if I can interpret it.'

'Oh, don't you know Latin?' asked Vincent in mock surprise. Then he muttered under his breath: 'You seem to know everything else.'

'It's not Latin, it's Quodlatin.'

'Sounds like the same thing to me.'

'If only!' Folly laughed. 'Quodlatin is a *Lingua Fallax*, a language of deceit, full of riddles and double meanings. I know a little but not nearly enough. It takes years to learn it properly.'

As she spoke she was turning the delightfully crackly pages almost reverentially. The paper was so thin that there were nearly a thousand pages, some of them still uncut. The margins were annotated in minuscule characters in ink and pencil. She pointed to an ink drawing of a man. He held a pendant in his hand and a repulsive creature cowered before him.

'Kamptulicon had a pendant,' recalled Vincent. 'But it was dull, not a jewel.'

'I know,' said Folly. 'The pendant controls the Lurid – I'm sure of it.' She read the words below the picture. '*Calx Flutans Maris.* I think, but I'm not completely sure, that it means, "Drifting stone of the sea". If I can get one of these stones, then I can control the Lurid—'

'But stones don't drift.'

'It's Quodlatin. It could mean lots of things.'

'OK, so if we don't know what it is, then how are we going to find it?' There was no mistaking what Vincent thought of the idea.

'Easy. Kamptulicon has one. You're a thief; you can steal it.'

'Who told you that? I never said.'

Folly snorted. 'Come off it, Vincent. Ordinary people don't have secret compartments in their boots, or ten pockets in their cloaks.'

A smile played around Vincent's lips. 'Fifteen pockets, in fact, can be confusing, and to be precise I'm a picklock. They called me the "Pilfering Picklock" in the last place. What about you? What do you do?'

'I'm a hunter, like my father,' replied Folly without hesitation, almost as if rehearsed.

Explains the rabbits, I suppose, thought Vincent. He looked at his metal hand. 'But you're right. I suppose I could give it a try.'

'Good,' said Folly bluntly. 'Your life depends on it.'

CHAPTER 18
BODY OF EVIDENCE

Edgar sat stiffly in the Troika, a glass of Grainwine in his hand, trying not to drink it all in one gulp. There was an air of expectation in the aphotic carriage.

'Dr Ruislip has seen her, sir,' said Edgar to his concealed companion, 'and she cannot be persuaded; she wants to go before the judge. I think that she knows more than she is letting on. She could make trouble in the courtroom if the public hears what she has to say.'

'Then we will have to make sure they don't. Don't fret, Edgar – I didn't get to where I am without making friends in high places. I know a judge who will listen to what I have to say.'

'Excellent, sir. But what about the . . . er . . . body?'

'All in hand. Now, our business is concluded. We will meet again when all of this unpleasantness is over.'

Edgar knew that this was his cue to leave. He drained his glass and jumped out of the Troika, climbed into his own less luxurious Phaeton and drove away.

Chapter 19
The Reluctant Burglar

As Jonah walked away from Citrine's cell he was greatly troubled. He felt in his pocket for the sequentury that she had given him at their first encounter. Who would have thought that events would turn out like this? He did want to help her, but how could he be sure he would be doing the right thing?

Jonah might not have been a Degringoladian by birth, but as a sailor he was no stranger to superstition. He had embraced the ways of his adoptive city like a native, and as he hurried away from the penitentiary he too avoided the cracks and brushed the touchstones. He entered Mercator Square and made his way to Suma Dartson's black wagon. He put one foot on the step, causing the wagon to shake slightly, and knocked gently on the door with his large knuckles.

'Is that you, Jonah Scrimshander?' Suma's head appeared out of the window. 'What a lovely surprise!' Seconds later the door opened and she beckoned him inside.

'Is it really a surprise?'

Suma tapped the side of her nose with a conspiratorial grin and pulled the door shut.

Jonah's size was such that he filled the narrow doorway, but the interior of the wagon was surprisingly spacious. He looked at the carved cachelot teeth on the shelf and felt a mixture of pride and shame. Suma noticed. 'You mustn't feel guilty, Jonah. What's past is past. Those teeth are a reminder to you that you have changed. And there is no denying the artistry in your engraving.'

Jonah flushed. 'Where's the Mangledore?'

'I gave it away to someone who had need of it. Now, is there something worrying you?'

'A prisoner in the penitentiary has asked me for help.'

'The Capodel girl?'

Once Jonah would have been amazed, but now such prescience was what he had come to expect from the wily old woman. 'Do you think she is innocent?'

Suma shrugged enigmatically. 'Shall we ask the cards?'

Jonah nodded. He should have known better than to ask Suma directly for advice.

He set a small table between them while the card-spreader retrieved a box from under her chair, out of which she took a deck of cards. Suma's cards were decorated in brown and black, and Jonah had learned not to look at them for too long because the pattern seemed to come to life and confuse his eyes. Suma turned down the light; then Jonah took the dice and tumbled them across the table. Suma noted the number of scores and the symbol – the corvid again – deftly shuffled the cards and spread seven on the tabletop's soft purple baize in the shape of the winged creature.

'Choose two,' she said.

Jonah picked his cards, one from each wing, and placed them face down on the table. Suma turned them over and laid them side by side. 'We have truth – see the corvid and the scroll – and we have the Carnifex at the gibbet.'

Jonah leaned forward. 'Truth is in the noose? I don't understand.'

'I'm going to choose another card for you,' said Suma. 'It might help, but equally it might just muddy the waters.' She took a card from the corvid's head and turned it over. 'The Maiden,' she said.

'It's Miss Citrine,' said Jonah. 'It has to be. I am to help her. I know I am.'

Suma raised an eyebrow. 'I suspect you did not really need the cards to tell you that.'

By the time Jonah returned to the penitentiary Citrine had convinced herself that this kind, disfigured Cachelot hunter was her only hope of finding some way out of what had become a nightmare of gargantuan proportions. She thought that he believed her, she could see it in his eyes, but she knew he needed some real proof of her innocence. And that was outside the penitentiary walls.

As soon as she heard the grille slide across she ran to the door. 'So, will you help me?' she asked breathlessly before Jonah had a chance to say a word.

He nodded and Citrine let out a yelp of excitement. 'Shh,' he hissed. 'Yes, I'll help. I've had my cards spread and they have shown me that it is the right thing to do. Suma said she knew you well.'

'You've seen Suma?' Citrine could feel tears welling up in her eyes.

'Yes, but, listen to me, you can't rely on the judge to save your skin. If Edgar can pay off Fessup, he can sure as fish-bones pay off a judge. He wants you well out of the way.'

Citrine wiped at her eyes with her sleeve. 'If we can't trust the DUG or the judge, then who can we trust? Maybe Governor d'Avidus – my father always spoke well of him. Could you go to him and plead my case? Look, take my Trikuklos, it's in a shed, there's a key in the wall, I have money, in the house—'

Jonah looked shocked. 'Hold your oars, Miss Citrine. I'm no thief. I don't know if I can.'

The sound of voices and loud laughter caused them both

to look up. Citrine felt cold fear. 'Who is it, Jonah? What's all the noise?'

Jonah craned his head back and looked up the corridor. 'Aw, catguts. It's Edgar and Fessup and . . . oh no!'

'What is it? What's wrong?'

'He's with an officer of the court.'

'What does that mean?'

'Never anything good,' Jonah muttered.

The party of three arrived at the cell, led by Fessup. 'Open up, lad,' he ordered.

Begrudgingly Jonah opened Citrine's cell door and the officer of the court, a weaselly, greasy-haired man, stepped through it and began to read from a piece of stiff paper. His voice was monotonous, utterly lacking in emotion, but the news he delivered couldn't have been more shocking.

'Citrine Capodel, you have been tried in your absence in a court of law and found guilty of one count of murder. You are to be taken from this place this evening and hanged by the neck until dead.'

CHAPTER 20

THIS EVENING'S ENTERTAINMENT

PUBLIC HANGING

TONIGHT AT 12 NOX AT QUADRIVIUM CROSSROADS

Miss Citrine Capodel will be

Hanged by the Neck for the

HEINOUS CRIME
OF
MURDER

ADMISSION 1 SEQUART (GUARANTEED NO MORE
THAN 15 FEET FROM THE GALLOWS)
LICENSED FRUIT AND VEGETABLE SELLERS ONLY

'Citrine Capodel?' murmured Vincent, stopping to read one of many hastily pasted-up posters that now competed with festival bunting around Degringolade. 'Well, well. Looks can be deceiving.'

'You know Citrine Capodel?' asked Folly, unable to hide her surprise.

'Oh yes,' said Vincent, secretly pleased. 'Before I met you and got mixed up in all this business.' He waited for her to react, to say no doubt that she too knew the Capodels, but she said nothing. 'At 12 Nox, eh? Isn't that a bit late for a hanging?'

'Not around here,' Folly said grimly. 'They'll throw the body into the Tar Pit just in time for the Ritual of Appeasement.'

It was already Nox, and Vincent and Folly were on their way to Mercator Square. Having agreed to help Folly steal Kamptulicon's pendant, Vincent had spent the remainder of the day in the Kryptos being versed by her in the finer points of Lurid repulsion. Now his cloak of many pockets was bulging again; not with the usual spoils, however, but with Lurid deterrents – in particular bags of dried black beans.

'Black beans distract Lurids,' Folly had explained. 'You can use other seeds or grain, but black beans are the most effective. They've been used for centuries to repel evil spirits. Lurids are compelled to gather them up. Just throw the bag, and as soon as it hits something it will burst and scatter the beans in all directions. There's a small amount of explosive in the middle. Keeps Lurids busy for ages! Actually, that's how

I got into the shop to rescue you. I used a charge from one of the bags to destroy the lock. And Kamptulicon was in such a hurry to get to you he left the trapdoor open.'

Very lucky, thought Vincent.

Now as he walked along he could feel the Natron disperser he had tucked into his belt digging into his side. It resembled a flintlock pistol but with a shorter, fatter barrel. It was simple to operate: you filled a chamber with natron, pointed it in the direction of a Lurid and squeezed the trigger. Natron was an exotic form of salt, he had learned, and was far more effective against Lurids than brine crystals from the Turbid Sea. It caused a more intense burning and kept them at bay for much longer. Folly had used both black beans and Natron when she had rescued him from Kamptulicon.

Last but not least, she had given him a handful of stunners, the third weapon in her anti-Lurid arsenal. These walnut-sized nuggets could fit in the palm of a hand, yet were powerful enough to fell a grown man. Kamptulicon had been laid out on the cellar floor by a stunner.

Now, as they approached Mercator Square, Vincent noted that the wailing was much louder than before, and somehow it sounded different. Folly seemed immune to it, but it set his teeth on edge. She entered the square first, but almost immediately Vincent grabbed her by the arm and dragged her back to the safety of the alley. 'Spletivus!' he oathed.

'Kamptulicon's done it – he's freed them all! What in Aether are we going to do?'

And, indeed, it did look as if Kamptulicon had been hard at work; Mercator Square was thronging with scores of monstrous wailing Lurids.

Folly wrested herself out of his grasp. 'Calm down, they're not real,' she said with a hint of a smile. 'They're people in costume.'

Vincent dared to look again and saw that she was right. The Lurid-like forms wandering between the stalls were in fact just Degringoladians dressed in rags, brandishing sticks and what looked like long-handled tridents. The wailing came from under repulsive blood-streaked masks, with huge bloodshot eyes and gawping mouths with broken discoloured teeth.

'It's all part of the festival,' explained Folly. 'Tomorrow morning is the Ritual, but traditionally, the day before, people dress up and parade around the square. It's a sort of warning to the Lurids that the ritual is close. And of course now there is a hanging for them to go to.'

Vincent chewed on his lip. This city was really stretching the limits of his tolerance. The sooner he got out of Degringolade the better. He looked down at his metal hand and saw how the yellow streetlights turned its polished surface to gold. He was already proficient at operating the fingers, and Folly's

Antikamnial and soothing balms were very effective pain relievers; in fact, he hardly knew the wound was there. But another part of him, deep inside, ached like a pressed bruise every time he envisaged the mangled hand beneath the metal. And his jaw clenched when he thought of what he would like to do to Leopold Kamptulicon. His time would come.

Folly was already pushing her way through the noisy crowd to the other side of the marketplace and he had to run to catch up with her, passing Suma Dartson's wagon on the way. As he took one final look back at the bizarre throng he was certain he saw the curtain at the wagon window twitch. He hurried after Folly down the maze of side streets and alleys that led to Kamptulicon's shop.

At the top of Chicanery Lane Folly held up her hand for Vincent to stop. The lamp-shop sign was swaying slightly in the breeze and the mere sight of it turned his stomach. He had not forgotten, and wouldn't for a very long time, the stench of the Lurid and the taste of its rotting lips. He patted his weapons for reassurance, steeling his nerve for whatever challenges or horrors might lie ahead. But his mouth was dry and he licked his lips nervously. Folly was watching him closely.

'As long as there's no one in the shop, you pick the lock and we'll go in,' whispered Folly. 'If Kamptulicon's down in the cellar, we can draw him out. You deal with him – use a stunner – and I'll attend to the Lurid. I can hold it off long enough for you to get the pendant.'

'What if Kamptulicon's not wearing it?'

'He will be. It's his only means of controlling the Lurid; he's not going to let it out of his sight. Once we have the pendant, the Lurid will be under our control. Well, mine actually, seeing as only I know the Supermundane words.'

Vincent raised an eyebrow. The plan was simple enough, perhaps too simple, and Folly's confidence, far from being reassuring, was actually disconcerting. 'Remind me how, exactly, you know all this.'

'From the book, of course,' said Folly without hesitation. 'How do you think?'

Vincent didn't know what to think. His thief's instinct was sending out warning signals loud and clear. It had all seemed very straightforward in the comfort of the warm Kryptos. Picking the lock was simple, and even the prospect of Kamptulicon wasn't particularly worrying. But the Lurid, that was another matter. He had not had to consider such obstacles before; usually when he was at work the inhabitants were asleep. But this was Degringolade – anything could happen. 'I'm a thief, not a damned Lurid hunter!'

Folly shot him an odd look and he realized he had just spoken this last thought aloud. 'Focus first on what is most important,' she urged, 'the pendant. And then if we work together we can both get what we want.'

They checked that the street was empty and on stealthy feet approached Kamptulicon's shop. Vincent dropped to a crouching position, Folly did the same, and they crawled along under the low windowsill. Vincent dealt swiftly with the first lock, but was somewhat galled to find that the other two were already open, destroyed when Folly broke in. He knew she was watching his every move and there was no denying he wanted to impress her. He opened the door and slipped through the narrow gap without a sound. Folly crept in behind him, her feet scraping on the floor, and he took a certain amount of pleasure in shooting her a look of disapproval. They moved quickly through the dark interior to huddle behind the counter. Folly folded back the rug to reveal the trapdoor. She pulled at the ring before Vincent could stop her. and to his surprise the trapdoor began to open.

'It's not locked,' whispered Folly, and she opened it all the way. 'Better I go first,' she mouthed. 'In case we meet the Lurid. It's not after me, remember.'

With a queer mixture of reluctance and relief, Vincent had to agree, and he signalled to her to go down the steps. Folly lit her manuslantern, turning the flame as low as possible, and began to descend.

Vincent brought up the rear very warily. All the nights he

had shimmied up drainpipes and scampered across rooftops and crept around people's houses, he had never felt fear like this. He could see Folly up ahead in the narrow tunnel. She looked back at him, and the way the light fell on her face gave her the appearance of a sunken-cheeked ghost. She smiled and then she disappeared from sight. There was an ominous silence. Suddenly the tunnel was lit up in white and he heard an anguished cry.

'No!'

Vincent raced forward, a beanbag ready in his raised hand, and skidded around the corner into the chamber. But there was no need for his haste. Folly was standing alone by the cold fireplace, her arms hanging limply by her sides. A large lamp on the table was the source of the light.

'Kamptulicon's gone,' she said incredulously. 'He's taken everything and gone. I'll never get him now.'

Him? wondered Vincent. Does she mean the Lurid or Kamptulicon?

CHAPTER 21
A CLOSE SHAVE

'Murderer! Murderer!'

Citrine covered her ears to block out the shouting. She was huddled up in a metal cage on the back of the gallows cart rattling towards Quadrivium Crossroads. At Mercator Square they had been joined by a crowd of chanting ghouls with blood-streaked faces, brandishing sticks and tridents. They were following still, battering at the sides of the cage, the metal bars ringing out under the assault. She felt something landing on her, something soft and wet: a rotten tomato. She wiped it away and fought back tears.

'I'm innocent,' she cried out at the jeering crowd, but they only laughed louder and the onslaught continued. The driver seemed to take great delight in travelling at a snail's pace to ensure that the mob could keep up the tirade of abuse. Then the cart turned sharply, throwing Citrine sideways, and when she righted herself she was greeted with the sight she had been dreading: the unforgiving gallows at Quadrivium Crossroads. And right before it, feet splayed, hands on hips and eyes peering out from behind his black mask, stood the Carnifex, the anonymous hangman of Degringolade. Lined up on the gallows crossbeam she saw the jagged silhouette of a flock of corvids, jostling for position, croaking harshly.

There must be two score there, thought Citrine. Waiting to pick me clean!

Things had moved quickly once the officer of the court had announced that Citrine was to be hanged. As Jonah looked on helplessly she had been taken away and placed in solitary confinement in a holding cell for those condemned to death. She had struggled all the way, demanding to know how this had happened, how she could have been convicted without a chance to defend herself, but the guards' expressions were impenetrable. She could only assume that Edgar's purse strings were longer than she had thought.

As Nox fell she was taken to the penitentiary courtyard and pushed roughly into the gallows wagon. There was straw on the floor of the cage and stains of a most repulsive nature. She sat with her back against the bars to steady herself and drew her knees up to her chin. She felt as if, in a matter of moments, she had been catapulted from one life to another.

Now, as the wagon rolled along, she took in the familiar sights of the city for the last time, and its beauty was tempered by the ghoulish bunting for the Festival of the Lurids. She thought of Suma Dartson. The cards had said that something would be stolen from her. 'Fool that I am,' she murmured, 'I thought it was my Brinepurse, but it was my life.'

The faraway moon was still high above Collis Hill and her heart skipped a beat when she saw the unmistakable silhouette of the Capodel Townhouse. Could it really be true that she had once lived there? It seemed an age ago now. Was she really to die without knowing what had happened to her father? Oh, Edgar, she thought. What wickedness you have committed in your quest for silver.

Now, staring at the seven steps that led to the hanging platform, it took all her strength not to break down. The baying crowd was gathering behind the rope, their bloody masks and menacing weapons presenting a vile spectacle. Had they too gone mad like the Lurids as the moon retreated?

The driver flung open the cage and reached in. Citrine clung to the bars but he pulled her so hard that she thought her arms would come away from her shoulders. At last she had to let go and he dragged her out. Edgar was waiting at the bottom of the steps with Dr Ruislip, Mayhew Fessup and two jailers from the penitentiary.

'Goodbye, dear cousin,' said Edgar solemnly. He choked

on a sob, or was it a laugh? Citrine could not tell.

The jailers pushed her up the steps before she could respond and passed her over to the muscle-bound Carnifex. He fixed the noose around her neck. 'Any last words?' he asked gruffly, holding the hood in his hand.

Citrine looked at Edgar. The mob quietened; they wanted to hear her deny her crimes, as those about to hang invariably did.

'Edgar,' she beseeched hoarsely, 'why are you doing this to me? Think of Hubert. He would not want this. Whatever it is you have done, I forgive you. I can help you. Please.'

Edgar, his pale face shining in the moonlight, shook his head slightly. He looked as if he was about to speak but then he turned away.

'You coward,' screamed Citrine, finally losing her tenuous grip on self-control.

'Enough,' said the Carnifex, and he tightened the noose around her neck. 'It's too late for that sort of talk.'

Citrine felt the roughness of the thick rope scratching against her skin. The Carnifex pulled the hood over her head. It smelled of dirt and sweat and, though she had not thought it possible, fear. In the absence of sight her hearing took over; she could identify every single sound: a cat walking along a nearby rooftop, the beating of an owl's wings as it crossed the night sky, the scratching of the corvids' talons above her

141

head. And Edgar and his conspirators shuffling their guilty feet in the dirt in front of the platform.

The Carnifex clasped the lever with both hands. The crowd drew a collective breath of anticipation. Citrine heard a creak as he pulled the lever back slowly. Hope was gone. She screamed, a great cheer went up, and the ground fell away from under her feet.

But, instead of the neck-breaking jerk she was expecting, there was a rapid hissing noise, a falling sensation and then she landed in a crumpled heap on the ground beneath the platform. Almost immediately there was another sound, a sort of swooshing and rattling, and it was a sound that Citrine knew.

The Trikuklos.

There began a great commotion: shouting, scuffling in the dirt, thuds, angry cries, feet running in all directions. A small ray of hope dared to flicker in her shrunken heart. The hood was pulled from her head and to her utter amazement she found herself staring into Jonah's scarred face. It was the most beautiful sight she had ever seen.

'Run!' he said. 'To the Trikuklos!'

And together they scrambled out from under the platform, leaped into the miraculous vehicle of salvation and pedalated away.

*

Vincent looked around Kamptulicon's secret cellar and saw with astonishment that the shelves that had once been so full were practically empty. The table that had been groaning under the weight of the madman's paraphernalia was cleared, apart from a few empty bottles and jars. His heart felt like a piece of lead in his chest. 'I suppose it's too much to hope that he left my smitelight.'

His gaze fell on the torture chair and his stomach lurched. He would have liked to see Kamptulicon sitting in it. As he walked around the room, searching for anything might be useful, out of the corner of his eye he thought he saw Folly take something from the table and put it under her coat.

'What did you find?'

Folly shook her head. 'Just a pot of balm. Could be useful.' She looked bitterly disappointed and Vincent began to think that this Lurid hunt was more important to her than he had realized. In the corner where he had tried to hide from Kamptulicon he stumbled on something in the darkness. 'My Mangledore!' he exclaimed. And indeed there it was, on the floor between the tea chests. 'It must have fallen off my belt.'

'You have a Mangledore?' Folly said from the chamber doorway.

'Surprised, eh? Suma Dartson gave it to me. Lucky I found

143

it. Now I don't have to rely on my wit and talent alone.'

'Funny,' said Folly, equally sarcastically. 'In my business I need all the help I can get.'

'What business is that?'

But Folly had already left.

When Vincent emerged into the shop Folly was waiting for him at the door. 'Might as well take some tar while we're here,' he said. 'I'm not used to coming away empty-handed.'

Folly exploded. 'Domna! It's not my fault Kamptulicon's gone!'

Vincent took a step back, surprised at her outburst. 'I'm not blaming you,' he began hotly.

'I'm sorry,' she said quickly. 'It's just . . .' Her voice tailed off.

Vincent took down two cans of d'Avidus of Degringolade Tar Deluxe. 'Look, I know how you feel,' he said in an attempt at mollification. 'Do you think Kamptulicon's left Degringolade entirely?'

Folly shook her head and visibly composed herself. 'I doubt it. He still needs you if he's to have that Lurid under his thumb. The pendant will only keep it enslaved for a short while without a body.'

'So what happens if I just hide so it can't find me?'

'Well, if you manage to evade the Lurid for long enough,

then no one can control it and it becomes completely free to roam as it pleases.'

'Let's do that then,' said Vincent. 'Just keep out of its way and let it go.'

'No,' said Folly sharply. 'Lurids are evil, evil creatures. I must . . . It must be returned to the Tar Pit.' She opened the door. 'Let's get back to the Kryptos. We need a new plan.'

Quickly, wordlessly, they retraced their steps to Mercator Square, each contemplating in their own way the missed opportunity. The square was almost empty now; the masked people from earlier had gone and only a few stragglers remained.

'Perhaps if a stone is hollow then it might drift,' suggested Vincent to lighten the mood. He had been mulling over the riddle all day but was no closer to solving it.

'Or maybe I just translated it wrong.' Folly seemed distracted. She had her nose in the air. 'Can you smell that?'

Vincent sniffed. 'I smell tar. And something else.'

'Lurid!' they said simultaneously.

'Run,' urged Vincent, dropping the cans of tar. But Folly stayed where she was and Vincent had taken no more than three steps before Leopold Kamptulicon stepped out from behind a stall and grabbed him by the arm.

Chapter 22
The Lurid's Kiss

'Now, boy, let's finish what we started,' snarled Kamptulicon, pinioning Vincent's arms behind his back. Vincent struggled valiantly but to no avail; Kamptulicon had his forearm across his throat and was choking him. Out of the corner of his eye he could see that the madman was holding the pendant. The grey stone was swinging violently on the end of the chain.

'*Luride, tipsum monstrate,*' called out Kamptulicon harshly, and the Lurid, until now concealed behind the nearby stall, showed itself. It had changed since Vincent had last seen it, becoming a more monstrous manifestation than before, and its ravaged face was a mask of unexpurgated evil.

'*Assumate puer!*'

The Lurid swept forward and once again Vincent found himself staring into the creature's dead eyes. His nostrils were under assault from its gut-wrenching stench and his very heart was crushed by the weight of its evil intent. The Lurid loomed over him, its face contorting with rage, and Vincent, in his immobilized state, was utterly helpless. He heard an angry shout and Folly came rushing at full pelt towards them. She was holding something, a three-pronged silver weapon he hadn't seen before.

'Folly, I . . . !' he gasped, but Kamptulicon tightened his grip, crushing his throat, and he couldn't speak.

Folly raised the weapon above her head and made as if to stab at the Lurid but then, inexplicably, she too seemed rendered useless. Her arm dropped and she stood staring at the Lurid as if entranced by it.

Spletivus! Throw a beanbag, a stunner, spray the Natron! Vincent willed her silently, horribly aware that his very consciousness was slipping away.

A moment later, as if Vincent's desperate thoughts were a sharp stick prodding her, Folly came to life again and launched herself at Kamptulicon from behind. She clung to his shoulders, strangling him with his own cloak. At the same time she grabbed at the chain and tried to wrench it from his neck. Kamptulicon ran backwards, still holding Vincent, and slammed into the stall. Folly took the full impact of the collision, released her hold and fell to the ground.

'*Assumate puer, extemplum!*' screeched Kamptulicon.

Vincent was now fully in the Lurid's embrace. He could only stare into its black eyes, searching for the human he knew was once in there. From somewhere close by Folly began to scream.

After a wild, bone-jarring ride through the backstreets of Degringolade, Jonah, who had proved to be a skilled if reckless pilot, finally brought the Trikuklos to a standstill on the outskirts of Mercator Square. Citrine, who had been holding on for dear life, turned to her saviour and flung her arms around him.

'Oh, Jonah,' she cried. 'You saved me!' She hugged him until he began to complain mildly that he was being half squeezed to death.

'We're not quite out of the water yet,' Jonah continued nautically. 'You've escaped the gallows but Edgar will still be looking for you; so will Fessup and the entire DUG. You're a convicted murderer now, and I'm guilty of helping you. It'll be both our necks in the noose if they catch us.'

'Not if I can prove my innocence,' exclaimed Citrine, her old determination resurfacing. 'But we can't risk going back to the Capodel Townhouse now, that's for certain. We'll have to find somewhere else to stay for tonight.'

'I think we should get as far away from Degringolade as we can,' said Jonah, covering the pedalators with his broad feet. The three wheels began to turn again and he guided the vehicle up the street towards the marketplace. He looked at Citrine with a big grin. 'I've always wanted to drive one of these,' he said. 'I never thought I'd get the chance. And I'm still getting my sea legs!'

'You're doing tremendously well,' enthused Citrine, finally starting to calm down and very happy to be a passenger for once; she was still shaking from her near-death experience. 'But exactly how *did* you save me? I couldn't see a thing with that hood on my head. How did you get past all those horrible masked people, and the DUG?'

'Cowardly mob,' said Jonah sternly, flushing with embarrassment at Citrine's compliment. 'Hiding behind their masks. But they don't scare me! I just pedalated at them, head on like a ship into a wave. They ran for their lives.' He laughed. 'As for your cousin Edgar, I rode right over his leg.'

'What about the noose?'

Now Jonah flushed with pride. He reached behind him and brought round what looked like a spear attached to a long line of rope.

'My Cachelot spear. Best shot in the seven seas, they used to tell me. Well, I ain't lost the touch. I aimed at the rope and it went clean through it. It was chancy, but, by the barnacles, it worked!'

'It certainly did,' said Citrine. She wrinkled her nose. 'That smell, like rotten fish, is it the spear?'

Now Jonah looked a little uncomfortable. 'It's my trousers. They're my lucky ones, you see, the ones I was wearing when I was in the Cachelot. I reckon as they brung me good fortune then so I wore 'em tonight. Us sailors are a superstitious bunch.'

Citrine laughed. 'Who cares about a . . .' she began, but at that moment Jonah pedalated straight into a commotion of the most horrifying nature: Vincent and Folly's mortal struggle against Kamptulicon and the Lurid.

'Domna!' exclaimed Citrine. 'That boy's being attacked, by one of those masked people!'

Jonah, spurred on perhaps by his earlier victory, grabbed his spear and jumped from the still-moving vehicle, leaving Citrine to slide across the seat and pull on the brake lever to bring the machine to a halt.

'Stop!' cried Jonah, waving his hands and running towards the fracas. 'Stop, you filthy landlubber!'

He wasn't sure which victim to help first: the floppy-haired boy held down by the masked tatter-clothed assailant, or the blond boy who was struggling wildly in the arms of a shrieking lunatic. When the lunatic saw Jonah, he snarled at him like a dog.

'Begone,' he cried furiously, 'or you will forfeit your life!'

Jonah hesitated. At such close range he could see this was no ordinary confrontation. He looked at the pair on the ground and realized with a start that what he had taken for a mask was in actuality a real face. As he dithered, the repulsive attacker suddenly released the boy, stood up and started menacingly towards Jonah himself.

'Fish-guts,' muttered Jonah. He stood his ground, brandishing his spear, and stared into the abominable face. In that instant he knew exactly what he was dealing with, though he would not have thought it possible.

'Stay back, you . . . you . . . mucky Lurid!'

He took aim and was about to release his spear when, to his sheer amazement, the Lurid stopped and stood back as he had instructed. It looked all about itself in apparent confusion. The other man, his face a picture of absolute fury, let go of his struggling victim and strode towards Jonah and the Lurid, shouting, '*Assumate puer! Assumate puer!*'

Folly – whom Jonah had mistaken for a boy – now no longer at Kamptulicon's mercy, wasted no time. She dragged Vincent away from danger and helped him to his feet. At that moment, to compound the confusion, a loud screeching of brakes signalled the arrival of Citrine in the Trikuklos. She drew alongside the trio and threw open the door.

'Get in,' she called. 'Hurry!'

Vincent, Jonah and Folly clambered in and, before Kamptulicon's disbelieving eyes, they drove away.

'*Subside!*' Kamptulicon shouted at the Lurid, and started running after the Trikuklos. But he had hardly gone more than a few yards when he realized that the Lurid had disobeyed his order to remain behind and was also trying to follow the fleeing foursome. He whirled on the spot and thrust the pendant practically into the Lurid's rotten face. '*Subside!*' he screeched maniacally.

It was only when the Trikuklos disappeared around a corner that the Lurid finally came to a stop.

CHAPTER 23
A Turn-Up for the Books

Folly's Kryptos was feeling rather crowded. It was perfectly adequate for her, and it could accommodate a single guest without issue, but now she had two more – Jonah alone took up the space of two – and things were decidedly tight.

After her second daring escape of the evening Citrine had pedalated the Trikuklos with all her might while Folly gave directions to the Komaterion. Vincent, pale-faced and weak, was slumped on the back seat, with Jonah trying to revive him by the only means known to him, in essence a series of slaps around the face. Although the Trikuklos was very efficiently geared, it was not suited to the boggy terrain of the salt marsh and eventually its occupants had to dismount. There was a thick mist all around and the flickering blue corpse candles were out in abundance.

'Don't pay them any heed,' warned Folly.

Jonah pushed the Trikuklos; its wheels were set just close enough to stay on the narrow path, but more than once it came dangerously close to rolling off into the quaggy marsh itself. Folly and Citrine supported Vincent who, although now able to walk, was clearly struggling to keep up. When they reached the Komaterion the Trikuklos could not negotiate a way between the headstones and statues, so Jonah concealed it under cover of branches and brush near the gates.

Soon the three guests were sitting at Folly's marble table recovering from their various ordeals, each sipping gladly on a soothing and aromatic tisane of Folly's own concoction and dipping hunks of bread into bowls of slumgullion. Vincent removed his metal hand and unwound the bandage. It was bloodied from Kamptulicon's wrenching and he was about to throw it on the fire, but Folly took it from him. 'I'll boil it,' she explained. 'And it can be used again.'

Jonah and Citrine had finished their drinks by now and were looking around the Kryptos with interest.

Folly drained her own tisane and spoke. 'I think proper introductions are in order, and some explanations. My name is Folly Harpelaine and you are all very welcome to my home.'

Citrine spoke first. 'I'm Citrine Capodel.'

'We've met before,' Vincent reminded her with his special smile.

'Yes, I believe you have my Brinepurse.'

Vincent, his smile disappearing as quickly as it came, rejoined smartly, 'And I thought you were to be hanged for murder.'

'She didn't kill nobody,' Jonah chipped in protectively. 'I rescued her from the noose cos I believe she's innocent. The cards as good as told me.'

Vincent, more than a little put out by Citrine's apparent immunity to his charms, looked disparagingly at Jonah. His voice was rough and uneducated, and he smelled strongly of old fish and seawater. It was causing the atmosphere to become rather unpleasant, despite the countering effects of the tisane. Vincent tried to get a proper look at the lad, but he insisted on keeping his head down. He was broad across the shoulder and almost as tall sitting down as Vincent was standing. And for some strange reason his coat toggles appeared to be made from animal teeth. He did not look the sort of company a girl of Citrine Capodel's ilk would normally keep.

'Well, Jonah, how in Aether's heights did you persuade the Lurid to back off?' asked Folly. 'It was as if you had some sort of power over it.'

'That was a *Lurid*!' exclaimed Citrine. 'Good gracious me! Do you mean to say one of them has escaped from the Tar Pit? Was it with the old man?'

'The filthy stinker was trying to kill me,' said Vincent, strapping on his metal arm. Already, even after such a short time, he felt self-conscious without it. 'And that old man is Leopold Kamptulicon. He did this to me.' He held up his arm. 'He controls the Lurid—'

'For now,' interrupted Folly.

'And for some crazy reason he wants it to take over my body.'

Jonah looked surprised. 'Domne, so it's true. Lurids really can take on human form.'

Folly explained briefly how she and Vincent had tried to steal the pendant, and how Vincent had lost his smitelight to Kamptulicon, and about the drifting stones.

'We don't know what the stones are,' she finished, 'but if I can find out why the Lurid listened to you, Jonah, it might help us. What do you know about the Supermundane?'

'Supermundane?' Jonah laughed out loud. 'I know only about whales.'

For the second time Vincent noted the look of disappointment that crossed Folly's face. 'Maybe it was the smell from your trousers,' he said with a snigger. He was beginning to feel better, a dose of Antikamnial had taken the edge off the pain, and he didn't like all the attention this rough brute was getting. 'Never mind a Lurid – it's enough to put a fellow off his dinner. You should burn them.'

Jonah protested. 'I can't throw away my lucky trousers. I was wearing them when I escaped from the belly of the Cachelot.'

Vincent let out a small noise of irritation. How in Aether had he got himself tied up with this bunch? Folly he could deal with, she seemed a capable, resourceful sort, but the other two? Citrine was hardly his natural ally, more the sort he was used to robbing. And why wouldn't Jonah show his face? What did he have to hide? The Kryptos walls were beginning to close in and he was getting distinctly itchy feet. He was used to working alone, coming and going as he pleased; being cooped up with these strangers was bringing out the worst in him.

'So, Jonah, you want us to believe you escaped from the stomach of a sea monster unharmed?' he asked rather meanly.

'Not entirely unharmed.' Slowly Jonah removed his hat and Folly and Vincent saw his scarred face for the first time. They were both rendered momentarily speechless. Citrine talked to cover up the awkwardness. 'What shall we do about these trousers then?' she asked cheerfully.

'I'll change,' said Jonah. 'I have more in my haversack.' He pulled off the stiff briny garment and Folly took it and started to roll it up, her nose twitching at the smell. As she did so, a shower of what looked like small stones fell out of the turn-ups. 'Is that gravel?' she asked.

Citrine collected them all up, a sizeable handful, and held them under her nose. She sniffed hard. 'This isn't gravel,' she said. 'I think this is ambergris.'

To everyone's surprise, Jonah jumped on the spot with a whoop of delight and punched the air, his fist nearly reaching the ceiling. 'By the briny ocean,' he exclaimed. 'Floating gold! My turn-ups were filled with floating gold!'

Folly stood stock still, the trousers in her hands, and just stared at him. Vincent's ears pricked up. Had Jonah said gold? This was more like it!

'It doesn't look like gold,' he said.

'No, it don't, but it's worth a fortune!' enthused Jonah. 'These lumps are made in the stomach of the whale, from squid beaks and suchlike. Now and again the whales spew it up and it floats ashore.' He grinned. 'And sometimes it comes out of the other end, if you get my drift. I must've picked it up in me turn-ups when I was in the Cachelot's guts. Who'd o' thought it, eh? All this time it's bin in me lucky trousers.'

'But where can you sell it?' asked Vincent, getting straight to the point.

'To a perfumer, of course,' said Citrine. 'Jonah's "floating gold" is a very important ingredient in scent-making. My own perfumer was complaining recently that someone had broken into his shop and stolen his supply.'

Something to keep in mind for the future, thought Vincent. Out loud he said, 'Well, now we've cleared up that mystery, let's get back to business. Folly and I have to deal with my Lurid problem.' He looked over at Folly for a reaction, but she was deep in thought.

'And I have to prove my innocence,' said Citrine.

'You know I'll help you with that,' said Jonah firmly. 'But I ain't sure how. That cousin of yours is as slippery as an eel.'

'Family can be tricky,' murmured Folly, re-entering the conversation. Then, decisively, she said, 'I think for the time being the best thing to do is help Citrine.'

Vincent did a double take. 'Er . . . why?'

'Because Citrine and Jonah saved us, when we were in trouble.'

Vincent could hardly object; there was no denying he owed them a debt. 'I suppose,' he said with an air of resignation. 'But I need that Lurid off my tail, and my smitelight's very important to me; it's all I have of my father. The longer we leave it, the less chance—'

'I know, I know,' said Folly. She seemed preoccupied and was chewing on her lip. 'But I need to think about this, before we go off on a half-cocked search for Kamptulicon. Citrine, what do you need to do?'

'I want go home, to fetch all the information I have on my father's disappearance, anything that might prove Edgar's betrayal for definite. There's a safe in my father's study. Edgar put something of mine in there the other day. And there might be other documents too.'

'Then take Vincent. He tells me he's the expert in all matters of lock and key. Though I haven't seen much evidence yet.'

Vincent curled his lip at the dig. 'And what will you and Jonah do?' Suspicion was vellicating his heightened senses. Something was definitely up. Folly was distinctly anxious to get rid of him.

'Jonah can stay here with me and lie low,' she said. 'I'm going to look at the book again. Maybe I can work out what these drifting stones are.'

Vincent thought for a moment. Folly was probably right. And he could no doubt pick up one or two things for himself while he was in the Capodel Townhouse. 'There's one slight problem – what if the Lurid finds us? It's already tried to get me twice. What if it's third time lucky?'

'I've thought of that.' Folly was holding a rag and a small brown bottle. Vincent recognized it from the trunk. She tipped the bottle on to the rag and then wiped the oily liquid across Vincent's blistered forehead. 'This will confuse the Lurid. It won't be able to track you now.'

Jonah laughed. 'Smoked haddock! That stuff really stinks!'

Vincent made a face and looked at Citrine. 'Well, let's go now then; it's the middle of the night – everyone will be asleep.' He was almost daring her to refuse, but she was up and ready to leave in a moment.

'Excellent. Then take these, just in case.' Folly pressed upon them both Natron dispersers and beanbags.

'And the Mangledore,' Citrine reminded Vincent.

Not long after, and more than adequately armed against the Lurid, and indeed any other Supermundane entity that might be abroad, Citrine and Vincent crossed the threshold of the Kryptos and set off into the night.

Jonah, tossing his bag of ambergris up and down lazily in his large hand, watched Folly bid the pair goodbye and push the heavy door to. *So that's where Suma's Mangledore got to,* he thought to himself. *What a queer crew we are. A convicted murderer, a one-armed thief, a landed sea dog and Folly.* He didn't quite know what she was, but he had seen the way she held her knife, like a weapon.

He continued to watch as she moved around the Kryptos, filling her satchel with an odd assortment of items: a shallow dish, kindling, bottles and pots. Every so often she consulted a small black book, as if for guidance, but when she began stuffing Vincent's bloodstained dirty bandages into the bag he could remain silent no longer.

'What the barnacles are you doing with those?'

Folly didn't answer.

Jonah wasn't going to give up. 'Did that book tell you what those drifting stones are?'

'I think so,' she said evasively.

'Really?' Jonah was excited. 'But you said if you had them you could control the Lurid!'

Folly stopped what she was doing. 'It's not as simple as that. What I need to do is send it back to the Tar Pit. For that you need bones. You summon a Lurid with a bone, and return it with a bone.'

'Plenty of bones at the Tar Pit.'

'There's a catch; the bone has to belong to the Lurid itself.'

'Oh,' Jonah sounded deflated. 'That ain't gonna be so easy.'

'Exactly,' replied Folly. 'And we still don't know why Kamptulicon freed it in the first place.' She fastened the satchel and belted her coat. 'I have to go somewhere,' she said tersely.

'Yes, of course,' realized Jonah. 'We have to tell the others about the drifting stones.' He started for the door, but the expression on her face stopped him. Before he knew what was happening, Folly flicked the fingers of her right hand at him. He felt a stinging liquid spatter across his face and he was blinded. He staggered backwards, arms flailing, and overbalanced, hitting his head with a stunning blow on the slate hearth. Dazed and confused, he was vaguely aware of someone kneeling at his side. A ghost, he thought, before realizing the pale face and shock of white hair belonged to the girl. And, to confound him further, she was tying up his hands and feet.

'I'm sorry, Jonah,' she said in a very ghostly voice. 'I have to go alone. I'll explain later. Oh, and I need to borrow this.' She wrested the bag of ambergris from his hand and then was gone.

As his head cleared and the stinging in his eyes subsided, Jonah surprised himself with a laugh. 'Well, I'm blutterbunged!' he said to the emptiness. 'I didn't see that coming.'

CHAPTER 24

COLD STORAGE

Vincent stole a glance at his sombre passenger. She was pretty, with her green eyes, and she was undoubtedly courageous. Soon all of Degringolade would be baying for her blood, even Edgar, her very own cousin. He couldn't help thinking that had he been in her shoes he would have pedalated out of the town and never come back. He regretted his earlier rudeness.

Having pushed the Trikuklos across the marsh Vincent was now enjoying piloting it. His metal arm was proving no hindrance. In fact, it was possibly an advantage, enabling him to keep a firm grip on the handlebars as the machine shook and rattled over the rough terrain.

'By the way, I do have keys,' Citrine informed him. 'You won't have to break in.'

'As a wanted criminal, maybe you shouldn't go through the front door. And cover that hair – you'd be recognized from a mile away. Who'll be in the house?' Vincent's voice bristled with efficiency.

Citrine, startled by his brusqueness, pushed her hair under

her hood. 'Edgar, maybe. Usually he's at his club until all hours.'

'Servants?'

'No. My father always let them have time off for the Ritual of Appeasement. Edgar did the same, which surprised me a little.' Just then the Kronometer struck three. 'Nox is nearly over, not long now before the Ritual.'

'I'd have thought this ritual would take place at night,' said Vincent. 'Somehow midnight seems a better time, or whatever you call it here.'

'Usually it's 2 Nox, which is the middle of the night. But every few years the lunar apogee coincides with the Ritual, and then the Ritual takes place at the moment of apogee. Exactly 6 Lux.' Citrine shuddered. 'You know, if it hadn't been for Jonah, it would be my body offered up for the Lurids.'

Vincent made a face. 'Uurgh. So who will they offer now?'

'Most likely a cow, unless they hang another criminal before then.' She looked at him. 'You must think Degringolade a cruel place.'

'When you're dead, you're dead.' Vincent shrugged. 'At least, that's what I used to think before I came here.'

Citrine laughed and changed the subject. 'Tell me about this smitelight. Why is it so important?'

Vincent stared straight ahead, his face an inscrutable mask. 'My father gave it to me. He won it in a wager. A fellow had invented a safe lock that he said was unbreakable, but my father broke it. He made me promise never to lose it. I have nothing else to remember him by.'

Citrine made a wry face. 'I have plenty of things to remember my father by, but they're all at home.'

Vincent smiled. 'We'll soon fix that,' he said, and pushed harder on the pedalators.

They skirted Mercator Square. It was quiet now, with little sign of the previous evening's uproar; a mask or two lay on the ground and posters for the hanging fluttered about. 'The calm before the storm,' said Citrine with feeling, and pointed Vincent in the direction of Collis Hill.

Shortly after, they wheeled soundlessly through the door in the wall and into the grounds of the Capodel Townhouse. Vincent parked the Trikuklos in the shadows. Citrine made a brief examination of the stables.

'Edgar's horse and Phaeton are gone,' she whispered. 'The house is empty.'

'I shouldn't have bothered with this then,' said Vincent, and he pulled back his cloak to show the Mangledore. 'It only works on people who are asleep.'

Citrine grimaced. 'Personally I find Mangledores rather repulsive. But many believe in them. Besides, if Suma gave it to you . . .'

'I know, I know,' said Vincent. 'I'll keep it.'

He followed her into the house through the scullery door, shrugging off his disappointment at the ease of entry. It wasn't that the door would have presented a challenge, but Folly's gentle mockery had touched a nerve and a part of him wanted to show off his true criminal talents, if not to Folly then at least to Citrine. They entered the dark, warm kitchen and he cheered up a little. This was his domain, other people's houses. His skills lay not with Lurids and black beans. Plain honest thieving would do for him every time.

Citrine lit a candle.

'Spletivus!' oathed Vincent, before he could help himself. He had not thought that the humble kitchen could testify to a family's wealth, but even in this dim light he could see that the Capodel cooking quarters were enormous, with a broad, gleaming stove, a huge array of copper pots and a wealth of culinary devices hanging from walls and ceiling, some of which he had not known existed, let alone known their purpose.

With mounting excitement he followed Citrine up the servants' stairs and along a narrow corridor to emerge in the grand entrance hall on the ground floor. The house was truly the most sumptuous he had ever entered, legally or otherwise, and he couldn't help stroking the couches and feeling the curtains as he passed, savouring the sinking softness of the deep rugs.

'Are these all Capodels?' He was looking at the numerous

portraits that hung from the picture rail. Citrine nodded. Vincent had never known any family but his father, and yet in this array of stern faces Citrine could trace her ancestors back decades if not centuries. It stirred up unfamiliar feelings of envy.

They skipped lightly up the stairs, all the while under the watchful eyes of generations of Capodels, to reach the wide, galleried landing. Staying close to the wall – Vincent couldn't resist running his hands across the velvety wallpaper – they made their way to Citrine's bedroom.

'Wait here,' she said, and disappeared into the room. Vincent stood by the door, but after a few seconds, wholly unused to playing the part of guard, he slipped in too. Citrine was rummaging in the drawers of her dressing table. She filled a bag with her belongings: the green bag that held her cards, some clothes, jewellery and a purse of money – Vincent knew well the sound of sequenturies against sequins – and finally an envelope tied with black ribbon.

Downstairs again, Citrine led him to the study. 'The safe is hidden,' she began, as she closed the door behind them. 'Oh, you've found it.'

Vincent had indeed found the safe, concealed inside the drinks cabinet. He had removed the false back and was examining the dial on the metal door. 'Hmm,' he murmured. 'A Linus Alternating Lock, excellent for security.'

'But can you open it?' Citrine was looking over his shoulder.

Vincent smiled. 'Of course. I was trained by the best.' And with a flourish he opened the thick, solid door.

Citrine giggled into her hand. 'Edgar would be furious to see this. He changes the combination every week to stop me getting in.'

Vincent moved aside and Citrine took his place. She reached in and took the Klepteffigium and a handful of papers, legal documents and two sets of blueprints. Vincent shut the safe again and Citrine spread the blueprints on the desk.

'Can you hear that?' asked Vincent. There was a distinct humming sound in the room.

'Look behind the black curtain,' said Citrine with an enigmatic smile.

Vincent saw a curtain to the left of the desk and pulled it back. In the alcove behind it there stood a black cabinet with a soft metallic sheen.

'Kamptulicon had one of those in his cellar.'

Citrine frowned. 'I think you're mistaken. There's only one in existence. My father invented it.'

'It certainly looks the same. What does it do?'

'It's a Cold Cabinet. It keeps things cold. Father was very excited about it. He discovered a chemical that cooled air. He

169

said it would stop food rotting. He wanted every house in Degringolade to have one. He was going to make them in the Manufactory, but then, well, he went missing.'

'Perhaps Edgar made another one and gave it to Kamptulicon.'

'Edgar in cahoots with that madman? Surely not.'

'You know that the device Kamptulicon used on my hand had the logo of your company on it?' said Vincent. 'The three intertwined *C*s.'

'Oh,' said Citrine, and made a little moue. 'I didn't know. I'm sorry. Maybe Edgar *is* involved.'

She looked at the two blueprints again. 'Look, this is my father's original design for the cabinet.' She was pointing to the sheet on the left. 'His initials are in the corner. But this second one is different. I think maybe Edgar has redesigned it.'

'Maybe there's something in this one,' said Vincent, and closed his hand round the cabinet handle.

'What's that awful smell?' asked Citrine.

'That stuff Folly put on my head.'

'No, it's something else. Wait –'

But it was too late. Vincent had already pulled open the door. He let out an ear-splitting shout of terror.

For there in the cabinet, large as life, was Kamptulicon's Lurid.

CHAPTER 25
THE THIRD MAN

Folly stood a moment at Quadrivium Crossroads to catch her breath. She had run practically the whole way across the salt marsh. Above her the distant moon was perfectly round, hanging over Degringolade as if by invisible strings. Further down the road the dark outline of the city scored a jagged line across the night sky. A vibrant orange glow was now emanating from Mercator Square, causing the miscellaneous metals of the surrounding buildings to coruscate, and colouring the burnished steel of the Kronometer. The crowds were already gathering with their burning brands, preparing for the procession to the Tar Pit. She hadn't much time; the Ritual was due to start at 6 Lux, less than an hour from now.

At the edge of the Tar Pit Folly pulled on her gas mask and ran nimbly down the slope to the shore. In the middle of the dark lake the frantic Lurids were moving back and forth across the seething surface. The wind blew their melancholic wailing and moaning to her ears. There was no doubt in Folly's mind that they knew she was there. As they became more and more agitated so too did the black broth, bubbling and popping like pus-filled boils in a plague sufferer's armpit, a discordant accompaniment to the Lurids' lamentations. Folly thought the way the surface swelled and subsided was like the rising and falling of a monster's chest.

Ignoring the menace all around her, she walked quickly between the salt pillars and over the bony detritus on the shore until she found a relatively level spot that suited her needs. It was no more than a stride from the lake's edge and she was aware all the time of the long tendrils of tar creeping malevolently towards her.

She placed Kamptulicon's book on the ground, opened it at a dog-eared page and weighted it down with a rock. Or was it a bone? She didn't look too closely. She ran her finger back and forth across the page, her lips moving as she read the words, and then began; first she arranged a small pile of kindling on the ground, in a sort of lattice, and balanced the shallow dish on top. Next she lit a large clump of moss with a Fulger's Firestrike and pushed it under the sticks. They caught easily and she burned the tips of her fingers when she dropped the stained and stale-smelling bandages into the dish. She sprinkled them with helichrysum oil, sesame seeds and ground cumin. Soon the tongues of orange flame that already licked voraciously at the edges of the dish turned yellow and the bloodied cloth began to give off clouds of strong-smelling steam.

Finally Folly stood by the fire, holding the book in one hand, and began to recite the words on the page.

'*Luride, adeste mihi, soror sanguine, perfidelis, sponte.*'

And there she remained, an eerie figure swathed in swirling smoke, keenly observed by the stinking, baleful ghostly horde watching and waiting. One and all.

The Lurid in the cabinet shocked Vincent to the core. He leaped back like a scalded cat and it was Citrine who darted forward and slammed the door shut. She leaned up against it, bracing her feet on the parquet floor in front of her.

'Domna!' exclaimed Vincent, and he whipped out his Natron disperser. 'I'll count to three, then you open the door and I'll shoot it when it comes out. 1 . . . 2 . . . 3!'

Citrine wrenched open the door and jumped aside. Vincent planted himself directly in front of the cabinet, the disperser in one hand, a beanbag in the other. 'Come on out, you dirty stinker,' he cried. 'And I'll blast you to Plouton!'

But the Lurid in all its wretched decay remained exactly where it was, rigid and unseeing in the cabinet, and to all appearances as dead as it had ever been.

'Hah!' cried Vincent, and squeezed the disperser trigger, releasing a shower of Natron crystals, but at exactly the same moment Citrine ducked in front of him and shut the door again. The Natron sounded like rain against the metal.

'What in Aether are you doing?' hissed Vincent hotly.

'Maybe it can't come out,' said Citrine, brushing the crystals from her clothes. 'Without Kamptulicon telling it.'

'Well then, it's a sitting duck. I'll shoot it anyway.'

'But did you see how it looked? I mean it's young, not an old man like I thought it would be.'

'So? Don't tell me you feel sorry for it!'

'No, of course not!'

'Then open the cabinet. I just want rid of it.'

'But that's just it. We don't actually know how to get rid of it. The weapons only distract it,' Citrine argued. 'At least when it's in the cabinet it can't do us any harm.' Vincent was about to disagree again but Citrine put her finger to her lips and turned her head to the door. Vincent heard it too: voices and footsteps.

They spoke at the same time: 'Edgar!'

Hurriedly Citrine ducked into the alcove, squeezing into the gap between the wall and the side of the cabinet and dragging Vincent after her. The voices grew louder, the footsteps heavier. She looked up in horror. 'The curtain,' she hissed urgently. 'It's still open.'

Thinking quickly, Vincent slid the switch on his artificial arm, pointed at the curtain rings and moved his arm across the air. The metal curtain rings, by force of the magnet, slid simultaneously with his arm until the curtain was fully drawn. Citrine gave Vincent a nod of admiring approval. Then they shuffled into the space behind the cabinet and stood stock still, side by side, their noses only inches away from the oily coils that snaked back and forth across the rear of the machine. It was just tall enough to hide them if they bent their knees slightly. Seconds later the study door opened and they heard the ingress of at least two people.

'I can smell it already,' said a voice.

'Edgar!' mouthed Citrine to Vincent.

'Hmm,' mused a second, 'I'm surprised. Usually the cabinet contains the smell.'

'It's Kamptulicon,' Vincent whispered back. Then, before she could react, the curtain was drawn back with a flourish.

'Are you sure this is safe?'

'Completely,' replied Kamptulicon. 'I alone have the means to control it. The cold paralyses the Lurid and will keep it immobile until I find that blasted boy and finish the process. He's not a Degringoladian, I believe, but an outsider.'

'There are plenty of urchins on the street who wouldn't be missed,' laughed a third, deeper voice. Citrine and Vincent exchanged glances – who was this?

'Don't I know, sir!' said Kamptulicon. 'But the Lurid is bound to the boy so I have to use him. There are exceptions, as you know, but they're complicated. Besides, he knows too much now.'

'Won't the stuff on his head lead the Lurid to him? You said that's how you found him in Mercator Square.' This was Edgar.

'Yes, and if it hadn't been for your cousin and all that business at the gallows—'

'I couldn't help that! Mayhew Fessup and the DUG are on to her.'

A 'tsk' of irritation silenced them both. 'This is no time for your petty grumblings,' said the third voice. 'I've got to be at the Ritual soon. Oh, and the *Degringolade Daily* will be printing this tomorrow.' There was the sound of rustling paper and murmurs of approval. 'As for your cousin, I'll wager she is with the boy; find one, find the other.'

'That is exactly what I intend to do,' said Kamptulicon. 'Now, stand back.'

Vincent touched his forehead where Kamptulicon had smeared the binding paste and he was troubled. What if the Lurid could still detect it underneath Folly's oil? He only had her word that it would put the Lurid off his scent. Could he really trust her? Other, more worrying questions were starting to surface, but right now he had to ignore them.

Citrine seemed to sense his anxiety and squeezed his hand to comfort him. A sharp hiss and a rush of cold air around their feet told them that the cabinet door had been opened. There was a clicking noise and the humming became even louder. The smell of tar was strong, but not as strong as the smell of Lurid.

'On my word!' breathed Edgar.

'Well, well, Leopold! It's not often I say this, but I'm impressed.'

'Kew, indeed, but now, if you please, hold your tongues,' said Kamptulicon. There was a brief moment of silence and then the madman's voice rang out loud and clear. '*Luride, amok!*'

Citrine squeezed Vincent's hand so hard his knuckles cracked. Sweat oozed from his forehead and swelled into beads. But then someone let out a cry of alarm.

'I thought you controlled it!' hissed Edgar in a panic. 'Where's it going?'

'It must be the boy's scent – it's picked it up.' Kamptulicon could not hide his excitement.

'Then he is close by!' said the third man. 'Follow it, you fool!'

Vincent felt sick. Folly's liquid hadn't worked. Maybe this was what she'd wanted. He swallowed hard and steeled himself for what was surely now inevitable. He felt Citrine nudge him. She was holding a bag of black beans. He reached awkwardly into his cloak for the Natron disperser, his heart hammering like a blacksmith on an anvil. Would he be able to reload before the Lurid got to him? He couldn't escape it stuck behind here . . .

'*Adeste mihi!*' shouted Kamptulicon. There was the sound of skidding footsteps, a door slamming and then silence.

CHAPTER 26

BLOOD IS THICKER THAN WATER

The Lurid arrived first. Folly's heart quickened when she saw it hovering on the brink of the Tar Pit. Then it descended the slope, moving in that way peculiar to a Supermundane entity, and came rapidly towards her, weaving warily between the salt pillars. She felt for the bag of ambergris in her pocket, then placed her other hand on the hilt of the shining weapon on her belt. Now the Lurid was right by her. She stared directly into its eyes. It gave no sign that it had seen her but brushed past and went straight to the fire. It circled it, sniffing the air. Folly forced herself to look closely at it and she was washed over by an almost unbearable feeling of sadness. It was human-like, but no longer human.

Then in her peripheral vision she saw Kamptulicon. He was panting audibly and pulling on his gas mask as he ran awkwardly down the slope. He came crunching across the shore and drew up between her and the snuffling Lurid.

'You!' he said in angry surprise, his voice distorted by

179

the mask's filter. A short but recognizable strip of bandage was hanging over the edge of the dish.

'I see,' he snarled. 'Very clever, very clever indeed. You used Vincent's blood to draw the Lurid here. I should have known; a girl who carries black beans and Natron as a matter of course is hardly your average Vulgar.'

'There's a lot you don't know about me,' said Folly coolly. Her heart was thumping so hard she thought he would surely see her body pulsating to its beat. Surreptitiously she kept her hand on the ambergris. Kamptulicon held out the pendant and ordered the Lurid to come to him. And, although it obeyed, Folly could see that it was reluctant to leave the fire, as if torn between two forces. Kamptulicon looked around suspiciously. 'So, is your metal-handed friend hiding behind a pillar, about to take me by surprise?'

'I came alone.'

'Then tell me where he is and I'll spare you. I don't have time for your puerile games.'

'No. Give me the Lurid.'

Kamptulicon's eyes widened behind the large lenses of the gas mask and he snorted with derision.

'You can't stop me from taking it. I have the drifting stones,' said Folly. 'And I have more than you.'

Kamptulicon's face darkened as he struggled to contain his ire. Sarcasm dripped like treacle from his words. 'I commend you on your translation of Quodlatin. You have my book, I take it. But where, pray, did you get your drifting stones?' He took a step closer.

Folly planted her feet solidly on the shore. 'Stay back, I'm warning you, or I'll turn the Lurid on you.'

Kamptulicon held up his hands in a gesture of surrender but he kept coming. 'Don't be stupid, just give me the stones,' he wheedled. 'It's dangerous. You're meddling with things you don't understand.'

'I told you to stay where you were.' In one swift movement Folly whipped out Jonah's bag. '*O Luride!*' she called. '*Contrucida impuratus!*'

Kamptulicon froze but the Lurid ignored her.

'*O Luride!*' repeated Folly, louder, a hint of desperation in her voice. But the Lurid paid her not one iota of heed. Its allegiance was clear: Leopold Kamptulicon.

Kamptulicon took immediate advantage of Folly's confusion. He grabbed her arm, forced her to her knees and tore the bag from her grasp. He opened it and sniffed it and poured out a shower of small stones on to the ground. 'You've been tricked, you fool,' he sneered. He threw the bag away and twisted Folly's arm further up behind her back. Then he felt the pockets of her coat and took her beanbags and Natron and, with a cry of delight, retrieved his book. 'Who are you working with?

What would you possibly want with a Lurid?'

Folly cried out with pain but shook her head in defiance. Kamptulicon merely increased the pressure on her arm, forcing her face down into the sharp shingle.

'I can make you tell me,' he said simply. 'Vincent can attest to that.'

The gurning Lurid was hovering nearby, waiting for instructions from its true master. Folly looked at it and her eyes filled with tears. And she couldn't help herself; she whispered something. Kamptulicon saw her tears and heard what she said and visibly started, as if he had touched a kekrimpari generator.

'What did you say?' he asked in disbelief. 'You called it by name. You *know* the Lurid?'

Folly shook her head. 'No,' she moaned, but the quaver in her voice belied her denial.

Kamptulicon cackled ecstatically beneath his gas mask. 'Have you just admitted there is a blood connection between you and the Lurid? Oh, my dear, how kind of you to sacrifice yourself in Vincent's place.'

'I know the rules,' gasped Folly. 'The Lurid is bound to Vincent, not to me.'

'There's more than one way to skin a cat.'

Folly's stomach lurched. *He knows something I don't.*

Kamptulicon crowed on. 'Did you skip that chapter? The

one where it says, "A Lurid can assume the body of a blood relative, regardless of any other bond."'

As the full meaning of Kamptulicon's words became clear Folly felt as if her very soul was draining away.

'Is this Lurid your father?' teased Kamptulicon. He put his hand to his chin in a mocking gesture of consideration. 'No, he's too young. I can see that in its rotten face. Then who? *Your brother?*'

Folly flinched, a movement so slight she hardly knew she had made it, but Kamptulicon felt it. His grin grew broader, causing his mask to shift on his face.

'So, Axel here is your brother. How did I miss the resemblance! What an ignominious end he came to on the gallows. How embarrassing for you.' He dragged her roughly to her feet, held her by her hair and twisted her round to face the slavering Lurid.

'*O Luride,*' he called out. '*Assumate puella soror!*'

'No, Axel, no! It's me, Folly. Don't do this.' But her appeal fell on very dead ears.

Time chose then to slow its relentless passing, as if to allow Folly to savour her last moments. She became intensely aware of everything around her: the sound of the seething tar, the wailing of the Lurids and the sky.

How strange, she thought. It's too early for sunrise.

And then the Lurid came forward with its cavernous

mouth wide open. And behind them the sky was lit up in orange and red. A deep reverberating chanting grew in volume as the thousand-strong crowd of masked Degringoladians approached the Ṭar Pit for the Ritual of Appeasement.

Chapter 27
Whose Side Are You On?

It felt like an age, but was in fact only minutes, before Vincent and Citrine finally dared to emerge from their hiding place.

'Spletivus,' said Vincent. 'That was too close for my liking. I can still smell it.'

'Are they – is *it* – definitely gone?' asked Citrine.

'Yes.' The cabinet was empty so Vincent closed the door.

'Then let's get back to the Kryptos,' said Citrine anxiously. 'I can't believe what Edgar has got himself mixed up in. We've got to tell Folly and Jonah what's happened.'

Vincent looked uncertain. 'You know, I'm not so sure Folly is on our side.'

'Aren't you? She seems friendly enough to me.'

'You heard what Kamptulicon said, that the paste he put on my head attracts the Lurid. But Folly wiped oil on my head to put the Lurid off my scent.'

'She did that to protect you.'

'That's what she said, but if she knew all along that the

185

Lurid could track me, then why didn't she give me the oil before? Like when we were coming back from Kamptulicon's shop? When it attacked she didn't help me at first, just watched. When we were behind the cabinet I had this terrible thought that maybe she wanted the Lurid to find me. Maybe she's using me as bait.'

Citrine looked thoughtful. 'But why would she want it to find you and then the next minute stop it from finding you?'

Vincent shrugged helplessly. 'I don't know. I'm just saying I'm not sure she can be trusted. What do we really know about her? She lives in a tomb and hunts rabbits and reads Quodlatin. And have you seen that weapon she carries?'

'But she stitched your hand and gave you the arm.'

'I know; none of it makes sense, but something is wrong,' said Vincent, flexing his metal fingers.

'That third man, I think I've heard his voice before, but I can't recall where,' said Citrine. 'Maybe someone who came to see Father or Edgar.'

'He left this behind,' said Vincent, picking up a piece of paper. 'It's an article for the *Degringolade Daily* about the hanging. Look.'

Daring Escape from the Gallows

Reported by Hepatic Whitlock

Last night an event that is unprecedented in living memory took place at Quadrivium Crossroads. A convicted murderer, the noose in actuality around her neck, effected a daring escape from the hands of the Carnifex. And the escapee? None other than the notorious murderess Citrine Capodel!

As to the method of her absquatulation, one cannot but admire the outrageous audacity of its perpetrator. Among the crowd of witnesses to the event were Chief Guardsman Mayhew Fessup, Edgar Capodel (the accused's cousin) and Dr Chilebreth Ruislip. CG Fessup reports that an accomplice arrived on the scene in a Trikuklos. He pedalated recklessly through the crowd of onlookers, endangering the lives of one and all, and at the very instant the trapdoor was released this marauding pilot fired what appeared to be a whaling spear at the hangman's rope. The rope was severed, Citrine Capodel was free and the pair sped away in the Trikuklos.

This is just one more chapter in the shocking story of murder and betrayal that dogs the Capodel family. Earlier yesterday evening the body of Hubert Capodel, the businessman missing since the night of the Ritual one year ago, was discovered on the shores of the Tar Pit. It was identified by an engraved silver timepiece that miraculously survived the destructive power of the tar. The emergence of the body has now fuelled speculation that Citrine Capodel might also have killed her father.

Edgar Capodel released the following statement:

'Very soon I hope to draw a veil over this time of wretchedness. I am relieved that Hubert's body has finally been found. At Crex tomorrow he will be laid to rest in a private ceremony at the Capodel Kryptos in the grounds of the Capodel Townhouse. His will – which I believe to be the cause of my cousin Citrine's malicious malfeasance – has been read. Dear, generous Hubert left me his entire estate and appointed me Chief Executive of the Capodel Chemical Company for life. I cannot say why he left my poor misguided cousin Citrine out of the will. One can only wonder if he had some inkling of her murderous nature. As to whether or not she killed my uncle, I will leave that to CG Fessup to investigate.

'All Degringoladians know that Hubert Capodel was a great man. Nanyone could have imagined that he would come to such a dreadful end. I will

endeavour to honour his memory by standing tall at
the helm of Capodel Chemicals, steering the company
through the rough and the smooth waters of the future.

'Kew all for your good wishes during this most
difficult time for my family. In particular, I am most
grateful to Leucer d'Avidus, who has been unerring in
his support. I cannot think of a man more deserving
of the title "Governor of Degringolade" and I am
confident that we, the denizens of Degringolade, will
always be well looked after in his capable hands. I
am certain too that Chief Guardsman Fessup and the
members of the DUG will bring my wayward cousin
and her accomplice to justice.'

'So, your father's been found,' said Vincent. 'That's good, isn't it?'

Citrine's lip trembled. Her face was ashen, making her green eyes even more startling. 'I don't believe for a moment that it's my father's body. That will is a forgery and everything Edgar says is a lie. And this is just one more lie, to make me look even worse than I do already.'

Vincent asked quietly. 'But how do you know it's not your father's body?'

'Because of this,' said Citrine, and she reached into her bag and brought out a silver timepiece. 'This is my father's timepiece. He only had one. Edgar doesn't know I have it. He must have thought Father was wearing it the night he disappeared, so whatever they have found is a fake.'

'Domna,' said Vincent. 'Edgar really has it in for you.'

CHAPTER 28
PICK A CARD

As Jonah's sight returned he managed, by dint of rolling and shuffling, to reach his Cachelot spear where it rested almost out of sight against the side of the fireplace. Inwardly thanking Poseidon that Folly had not thought to take it with her, he manoeuvred himself into a position where he could use the spear's cuspidate head to saw at the cord that bound him.

Jonah made rapid progress – although no longer at sea, out of habit he still kept the weapon sharp – and as soon as one hand was free he discarded the tool. Folly had overlooked one important thing about Jonah: as a sailor he was a master of knots, and had no trouble at all undoing the rather basic overhand loops that she had used to detain him. He stood up and relished the feeling of blood rushing back into his limbs.

But he was still locked in the Kryptos. He tried to force the lock with the sharp point of the spear – a fruitless task. He even tried using one of the Cachelot teeth from his coat. He pulled with all his considerable might on the handle but to no avail. 'Fish-guts!' he burst out. 'I have been in the belly of

191

a Cachelot. Surely I can find my way out of a Kryptos!'

It soon became apparent that the belly of a Cachelot was infinitely easier to escape than his present confinement. Jonah resigned himself to the fact that he might be trapped until Vincent and Citrine, or Folly, returned. He wasn't sure which would be better. Citrine could do no wrong in Jonah's eyes, but Vincent he considered slippery as a flatfish. Any fellow who paid that much attention to his hairstyle was suspicious in Jonah's book. Not to mention how his eyes had lit up at the word 'gold'. Folly was responsible for his current predicament – but, in her defence, she had apologized for trussing him up, and was only 'borrowing' his ambergris. She had said she would return and he wanted to believe her. The fact that she had left various belongings behind (he had found a purse of money in her trunk) suggested that she was telling the truth.

Jonah paced the small room, feeling like one of the prisoners he had so recently guarded. Eventually he ladled the remains of the slumgullion into a bowl and sat at the table, fletcherizing each piece of meat to extract every last ounce of taste, and waited patiently. As a Cachelot hunter he was well used to waiting. He was just picking a stubborn remnant of rabbit from between his teeth with his fingernail when he was alerted by knocking at the door. Muffled voices on the other side called out, 'Folly! Jonah! Let us in.'

'Folly's not here,' he bellowed. 'I'm locked in.'

'Stand back,' replied Citrine. 'Vincent can open the door.'

There was a light scratching sound and then the door swung inwards. Vincent and Citrine tumbled in breathlessly. Citrine closed the door immediately and bolted it.

Jonah sniffed. 'You smell like tar, and something else.'

'Lurid,' said Vincent grimly. 'What happened to you?' He had spotted the frayed rope on the floor.

'Folly tied me up and took off.'

Vincent looked the large seafarer up and down with a sly grin. 'You're saying that Folly, a girl half your size, tied you up?'

'She blinded me first.'

Vincent straight away remembered Folly taking something from Kamptulicon's secret cellar: the liquid that had blinded him? 'Kamptulicon did that to me,' he said with a meaningful glance in Citrine's direction.

'Where did she go?' asked Citrine.

Jonah shrugged his huge shoulders. 'She took some odd things with her – bandages and that black book, and my ambergris. And she said she knows what the drifting stones are, so my guess is she's gone to find the Lurid.'

'Kamptulicon's looking for that stinker too,' said Vincent slowly. 'Maybe she's going to do some sort of deal with him. You say ambergris is very valuable?'

'*My* ambergris is.' Jonah grinned and dangled a small bag in front of the pair of them. 'Folly took a bag of stones. I . . . um . . . thought Vincent was likely to steal it, so I swapped it and hid it.'

Citrine, who had been silent until now, spoke up. 'I think it's time I spread the cards. Maybe they will provide some answers.'

'Now this I have to see,' said Vincent, concealing his annoyance at Jonah's deception and blatant slur on his character.

'Then let's do yours. I'm still too upset.' She handed him the dice. 'Throw these three first. Add together the number of scores and that's how many cards you choose.'

Vincent hesitated, regarding the oddly shaped dice with interest. 'Are these made from bone?'

'No, from maerl – calcified seaweed,' said Citrine, 'harvested from the riverbed where the Flumen meets the Turbid Sea. Suma gave me them as a gift.'

'She likes to give things away,' murmured Vincent, and rattled the pleasingly weighted maerl pieces in his hand and let them fall. They tumbled across the table and came to rest. All three onlookers stared down; each die showed a single vertical score across its uppermost surface.

'That means you can pick three cards. Now, throw the other one for the spread.'

Vincent rolled the fourth die, the thirteen-sided piece of maerl with the symbols, and it bounced scatter-fashion across the marble. It landed showing a lizard of sorts.

'Salamander,' said Citrine. Deftly she laid out ten cards in the shape of the creature. Vincent's hand hovered over the shape. Only a matter of hours ago he would have scoffed at the merest mention of card-spreading; now here he was looking for answers from the very same.

'Choose,' prompted Citrine.

Decisively he turned a card from the salamander's head and one from each hind leg. 'Oh my,' he breathed as the pictures were revealed. 'They're moving!'

'They're lenticular,' explained Citrine. 'The images alter depending on the light and the angle you view them from.'

'But what do they mean?'

'The first is the Cunningman.'

Vincent looked at the sinister figure of the old man staring up at him from the card. He had the oddest feeling that the man's eyes were following him, and he was certain the sneer on his face was curling even as he stared. 'Cunningman?'

'Suma told me about this one,' said Citrine. 'Cunningmen practise the Furtivartes – Supermundane ceremonies and rituals.'

'Like summoning a Lurid,' said Jonah.

Vincent made a small snorting sound. 'Sounds like magic

to me.' A part of him still didn't quite believe all this, but he couldn't deny that Degringolade and all its peculiarities was starting to get under his skin.

Citrine shook her head. 'It's not magic. Magic is sleight of hand, trickery. The Supermundane is very different.'

'That book he's holding, it's just like the one Folly took,' noted Jonah.

Citrine started. 'Goodness, Suma always says to look closely, but I've never seen that before. I think it's an Omnia Intum.' She explained quickly. 'It means "all things within". It contains recipes for Supermundane libations and potions.'

'A sort of Cunningman's handbook?' suggested Vincent.

'Folly's not a Cunningman.' Jonah snorted.

'But the book belongs to Kamptulicon. I stole it from his workshop.'

Citrine looked increasingly grave. 'Domna! If Kamptulicon is a Cunningman, Folly could be in terrible danger.' She clenched her fists and pressed them against the table. 'I should have realized before. I just didn't think. I was so caught up with my own problems.'

'What about the Maiden?' said Jonah, pointing to the second card. 'This time it must be Folly.'

But Citrine was poring over the last card, a stream of gold coins overflowing from a chest. She turned it this way and that in the light, and as it moved the gold coins lost their sheen and became dull. 'I think it's about deception, something that is pretending to be something else.'

'Like my ambergris. It ain't gold, but I can swap it for gold. Maybe those drifting stones Folly was talking about ain't stones.'

Citrine's face suddenly lit up. 'Domna! I've got it!' She turned to Jonah and her eyes were shining with excitement. 'Jonah, what if your pieces of ambergris *are* the drifting stones? They certainly look like stones, and, Vincent, you said that Kamptulicon's pendant was dull, not a jewel. That's why Folly took the ambergris. She worked it out. She's going after the Lurid. We have to help her.'

Vincent looked unsure. 'But she could be anywhere.'

'She's gone to the Tar Pit,' said Jonah suddenly.

Vincent raised an eyebrow. 'You can tell that from the cards? That's some trick.'

Jonah pointed to the empty hook on the wall. 'She's taken a gas mask.'

'That just leaves one,' said Citrine. 'But we need two more.'

Vincent grinned and he pulled from under his capacious cloak two brand-new gas masks, each painted with the Capodel family crest.

Citrine gasped. 'You stole them from my house!'

Vincent shrugged. 'Lucky for you I did. But I'm not going

anywhere without that stuff on my forehead and the real ambergris.'

'Not just a pretty face then,' said Jonah, and gave him a hefty pat on the back.

CHAPTER 29

ROAST DINNER

The large black and white cow looked oddly out of place, tethered as it was to a salt pillar at the edge of the Tar Pit. It lowed softly to the remote moon and kept lifting its hoofs, as if trying to rid them of the sticky tar that now covered them. Behind the cow scores of black-gowned and gas-masked Degringoladians were streaming on to the shore, waving their three-pronged forks, flaming torches aloft, and chanting. In front of the confused beast the cankerous Lurids had amassed at the very edge of the lake, shrieking foully at the gathering denizens.

'Even if Folly is here,' said Vincent, scanning the anonymous throng as it descended to the shore, 'we'll never find her.'

He was lying on his stomach on the brink of the Tar Pit, a short distance away from the main thoroughfare, flanked on either side by Citrine and Jonah. They were hidden by the marsh weed and their dark clothing. Before they set off Vincent had smeared his head – and everyone else's for good

199

measure – with Folly's oil and put the bottle in his pocket. Jonah had the ambergris and they all carried whatever Lurid deterrents they had been able to find in the Kryptos. Citrine had suggested that Vincent take the Mangledore.

'Suma gave it to you for a reason,' she'd said. 'It might come in useful.'

'Bit late for that,' he had scoffed, and left it on the table, ignoring Citrine's tutting. Leaving the Trikuklos outside the Komaterion, they had crossed the salt marsh and joined the masses heading for the Tar Pit.

'I'll admit,' agreed Jonah from his position beside Vincent, 'this is like looking for a pilchard in a sardine shoal.' His gas mask barely fitted over his head.

'That's not the worst of it,' said Citrine. 'The DUG are all over the place.'

Vincent and Jonah groaned. Citrine was right; although they were wearing black gowns like everyone else, the guardsmen were all wearing gas masks visibly stamped with the emblem of the force.

At that moment the Kronometer rang out the last quarter. Almost at once the crowd stopped their monotonous chanting, leaving the Lurids to fill the night air with their agonized keening.

'There's something happening,' said Citrine. 'On the podium. The ceremony is starting.'

All three turned their masked faces back to the Tar Pit and looked at the black-bunting bedecked podium that had been erected for the occasion. A man had taken the stage and was about to address the crowd.

'Welcome, my good people,' he began. 'We are assembled here at this fateful hour of early Lux, while the moon is in her apogee, to offer this creature to the Lurids, to show them that we understand their pain. It is not often that the moon is in her apogee on the last day of the festival . . .'

'Who's that?' asked Vincent. Like everyone else, the speaker's identity was concealed by his gown and mask.

'I think it's Leucer d'Avidus,' said Jonah. 'The governor always leads the ceremony.'

'Leucer d'Avidus?' repeated Citrine. She grabbed at Vincent's sleeve. 'Did you hear that? He said "assemled"; he left out the *b*.'

Vincent looked confused. 'So?'

'Remember the third man, in the study? He said "grumlings" instead of "grumblings".'

Vincent's eyes widened. 'Leucer d'Avidus, the Governor of Degringolade, was the man in Edgar's study?'

'Yes,' hissed Citrine, but before she could say any more another voice, a voice that was a lot closer, and unmistakable, took them all by surprise.

'Well, well. Who do we have here?'

It was Leopold Kamptulicon.

As one, Vincent, Jonah and Citrine scrambled to their feet. Kamptulicon, his cloak pulled close across his black tunic, was standing over them. Torch flames were dancing across his mask, reflected in the glass, and his eyes were shining.

'Hello, Vincent. How's your hand? I see you're making the best of it. And what esteemed company you keep. A couple of fugitives, if I'm not mistaken. You must be Citrine Capodel. And you –' he looked at Jonah – 'I'll hazard that you are the mysterious spear thrower. Not many escape the gallows in Degringolade. But someone's missing from your merry band. Ah, yes – Folly.'

'Where is she?' demanded Vincent.

'Why, right here,' said Kamptulicon. He stepped aside and there was Folly standing behind him. But there was something different about her, something not right. Vincent realized it first. She wasn't wearing a gas mask!. But that wasn't it.

'Oh my creaking timbers!' exclaimed Jonah.

'Folly? Is that you?' asked Citrine in horror.

'Spletivus,' oathed Vincent.

Folly didn't reply, merely stood motionless at Kamptulicon's side. In many ways she looked normal; perhaps her hair was a little whiter and her skin a little paler, but her dark blue eyes were now the dead eyes of a Lurid in a human body.

The stunned trio stood silent, rendered speechless with shock.

'Why the long faces?' mocked Kamptulicon. 'Does she not look happy? After all, she has got what she wanted – to be reunited with her brother. And I can tell you he is ecstatic to have a body again. Imagine, to have suffered the indignity of swinging from the gallows, to have your flesh pecked from your bones by those lousy corvids, but then to regain a human form. And so quickly! Why, he was only tossed into the pit a few days ago. The young ones are always the most grateful. Look at the rest of the wretched devils out on the tar. Some of them have been in there for centuries. Bitter to the core.'

Jonah took a step towards Kamptulicon. 'Give her back, you . . . you . . .' Words failed him.

'Keep away,' snarled Kamptulicon, 'or I'll set her on you. She'll kill you in the blink of an eye. I am her master now. She's utterly loyal to me.'

Jonah pulled out the bag of ambergris but Kamptulicon only laughed. 'Too late. Your ambergris will no longer work. And forget your beanbags and your Natron – all redundant now. Axel has a body.'

With a roar Jonah rushed forward, lifted Kamptulicon by his furry collar and began to shake him. 'I'll kill you!'

'Stop!' shouted Citrine, and she grabbed Jonah by the back of his coat. 'If you kill him, we'll never get her back.'

With a howl of frustration Jonah dropped Kamptulicon and pushed him away.

'You're not as stupid as you look,' said Kamptulicon, dusting himself down. 'Enjoy the ceremony, and your freedom, while you can. Fessup has you surrounded. I suggest you go quietly, for all your sakes.' He nodded towards the path, where three guardsmen were standing in wait.

'*Secuteme*,' he said over his shoulder to Folly, and without even a parting glance she walked stiffly after him towards the Tar Pit.

The guardsmen began to approach, their handcuffs out and at the ready. 'Come quietly now,' called one of them. 'No need for trouble.'

Jonah took Vincent and Citrine, and steered them behind him. 'Keep calm,' he hissed. 'I have a plan.'

The three stood firm and then, when the guardsmen were only an arm's length away, Jonah shouted out, 'Now!'

He leaped forward and grabbed two of the guards, one in each hand, sandwiched the third between them and pushed all three to the ground. Then he sat heavily on them, winding them and rendering them unable to speak. At the same time Vincent stuck out his artificial arm and with a loud rattling three sets of handcuffs flew towards him and attached themselves to his metal hand. Before the guards realized what was happening they were cuffed together, hands to feet and to each other.

'We've got to do something,' said Citrine urgently, searching for the handcuff keys and throwing them into the marsh. 'We can't leave Folly like that.'

'But what can we do? We don't even have the book.' Vincent was busy stifling the guardsmen's protests by tying their cloaks around their heads.

Suddenly Jonah jumped up with a shout, grabbed Vincent and began to rip at his clothes.

'Have you gone mad? Get off me!'

But Jonah didn't stop. 'Where is it?' he said. 'Tell me you brought it.'

'Brought what?'

'The hand, the Mangledore,' gasped Jonah, tearing Vincent's cloak from his shoulders.

'But I left it behind.' He was cowering from the onslaught and for a moment he thought Jonah was going to punch him.

'Wait! I have it,' said Citrine, and she pulled the macabre appendage out from under her cloak. She looked at Vincent. 'Suma knows,' she said simply. 'I couldn't leave it.'

Jonah grabbed it from her and without a word he took a running jump from the brink and landed on the shore below. Citrine and Vincent watched in amazement as the sailor barged through the crowd, pushing his way right to the edge of the pit. And then he stood there, beside the trembling cow, holding the Mangledore aloft, ignoring the cries of the confused onlookers and the outstretched hands of the Lurids.

Up on the podium Leucer d'Avidus stopped his speech. 'How dare you!' he began. 'Guards!' he called. 'Seize that scoundrel!' Immediately two Urban Guardsmen came rushing forward.

'Hey, Kamptulicon,' bellowed Jonah.

At the sound of his name, Kamptulicon, who was still making his way down to the shore with Folly, looked towards the commotion. When he saw what Jonah was holding he stopped short. He turned to Folly. '*Contrucida!*' he commanded. '*Confestim, contrucida puer!*'

Folly was instantly animated, as if shot through with a bolt of kekrimpari. She moved rapidly down the slope and on to the shore. The crowd gasped at the sight of her and recoiled from the invisible aura that surrounded her, sensing something unnatural, something of the Supermundane. Two guardsmen were upon Jonah, but he shook them off in one immense burst of strength and they fell into the tar. Then he waded out into the boiling broth, oblivious to the clawing, overwrought Lurids, drew back his spear arm and threw the Mangledore with all the force he could muster right out into the centre of the churning lake.

The Kronometer rang out and on the sixth chime, at the exact moment of the lunar apogee, the hand landed on the black surface.

The effect was instantaneous.

The yowling Lurids fled towards the sinking hand and gathered around it in one revolting congregation of festering decrepitude. The awestruck crowd, making noises of wonderment and paralysed by disbelief, watched as the Lurids seemed to take one huge breath. The tar retreated from the shore towards the sucking ghouls and swelled into a huge mass some ten feet high. Then, without warning, the black bubble exploded and spattered the shore and the throng with the foul, stinking brew.

Chaos descended.

Blinded by the tar, people started to shout and run in all directions, dropping their torches. Huge tongues of flame shot up as the tar began to burn. The Lurids' screaming reached an ear-splitting pitch. At the podium, Leucer d'Avidus was frantically trying to clear his mask.

Vincent and Citrine, still on the brink of the pit, watched the turmoil.

Citrine was the first to react. 'Folly,' she said. 'Look at Folly.'

Folly had just reached the shore when the Mangledore hit the surface. At the same moment she was stopped in her tracks as if she had come up against an invisible immovable object. Now she was shuddering violently, in the grip of an extreme mania. She dropped to her knees, her body arched violently and she threw back her head. The howl that came from her mouth was not of this world.

'Holy codfish,' muttered Jonah, struggling to escape the knee-high tar. He put his hands to his ears, as did the deranged crowd, as did Vincent and Citrine, as did Kamptulicon, until at last the scream ended and Folly fell forward on to the bony shingle. And then they all saw a most extraordinary sight.

There emerged from Folly's body, through her ears, her nose, her mouth, through the very pores in her skin, a sulphurous yellow smoke. And as it drifted upward it condensed into the shape of a Lurid and flew howling back to the phantom horde that had regrouped on the far side of the lake.

Now the fire was spreading fast, jumping from one pool of tar to another. People were fleeing wildly, dodging the flames, crashing into the salt pillars, scrambling up the slope, clambering over fallen bodies. Jonah finally staggered from the pit and made his way to where Folly lay inert on the shore. He knelt beside her, protecting her, until Citrine and Vincent appeared.

'Let's get the Aether out of here,' shouted Vincent over the cacophony.

Jonah gathered Folly in his arms and ran, ploughing a path through the crowd, Vincent and Citrine on his heels. At the top of the slope he stopped and set Folly down. Vincent and Citrine took her between them.

'Just one last thing,' said Jonah.

'No! We don't have time,' shouted Vincent above the pandemonium. 'Kamptulicon's right behind us.'

And indeed he was, striding towards them, recognizable only by the green lining of his cloak, which itself was barely visible, so splattered was it with tar.

'Exactly,' said Jonah. He took his spear from the pouch on his back and held it aloft. Kamptulicon froze at the sight. Jonah released the spear. The Cunningman tried to duck, but he was too late. The spear hit its mark, tearing through the hem of Kamptulicon's cloak, its lethal barbs snagging the material. Jonah pulled sharply on the line and the cloak was ripped from Kamptulicon's shoulders and flew back to him. He bundled it up and stuffed it under his arm. 'Now let's go,' he said.

And they ran for their lives from the hellish inferno behind them.

CHAPTER 30
DOMNA!

Once again the Kryptos was suffused with the intoxicating smell of tisane, but this time it was Folly who was being ministered to. She lay on her bed, her bloodless face framed by her tousled white hair. But she looked peaceful, for a moment at least, before she opened her eyes and sat bolt upright.

'Where's Jonah?'

'He's gone with Citrine,' said Vincent. 'How do you feel?'

Folly sat back slowly against the wall. 'Awful. Like a bottle that's been turned upside down and emptied.' She took the mug from Vincent and sipped. 'I can't really describe it. I couldn't speak but I knew what was going on.'

'Do you remember what happened?'

She frowned. 'Jonah saved my life. But how did he know – about the Mangledore?'

'A lucky guess, he said. He knew that Suma made it from the last body on the gallows, and when Kamptulicon let slip that's who the Lurid was he worked out the hand belonged to it. So he threw it in the Tar Pit, and the Lurid had to leave you and return.'

'The Lurid, my brother,' murmured Folly.

'Kamptulicon must have taken a bone from the gallows to summon it in the first place.'

'The leg was missing,' recalled Folly. 'I saw the body on the gallows, but I didn't know who it was.'

Vincent narrowed his eyes. 'Why do you carry a Depiction of Leopold Kamptulicon?'

Folly started and began to feel in her pockets.

'I have it,' he said, and showed her the creased picture. 'I found it on the shore of the Tar Pit, where Jonah picked you up.'

'My father gave it to me, so I would know Leopold Kamptulicon when I saw him. He's a Cunningman.'

Vincent sat back on his heels and looked at her expectantly. 'You know, everyone was right. Suma doesn't do anything without good reason. And I'm beginning to think that about you too.'

Red spots began to burn on Folly's cheeks, and not just from the tisane. 'You deserve an explanation.'

'All I want is the truth – about you and Lurids and Kamptulicon.'

Folly took a deep breath. 'Lurids are evil, whoever they were, and they need to be dealt with. When the Lurid grabbed you in Mercator Square I was ready to destroy it, with my Blivet—'

'The silver weapon?'

'Platinum,' she corrected. 'Then up close I saw it was Axel, my brother. How could I destroy my own brother! So I tried to get the pendant.'

'But then Jonah came along with his ambergris and we all ended up in the Kryptos.'

Folly took another mouthful of tisane. She was starting to look like her old self, still pale but no longer deathly. 'When Jonah said "floating gold" I realized his ambergris was the "drifting stone" from the book. I'd read about a ritual that used bloody bandages, so I knew I could get the Lurid to come to me. But I couldn't risk the Lurid finding you first – you were so determined to get rid of it . . .'

Vincent rubbed at his artificial arm. 'I had good reason!'

'So I gave you the oil to make sure it didn't come after you.'

'Why didn't you give me the oil before?'

Folly's face went even redder. 'I needed you to flush out the Lurid.'

'Bait,' said Vincent with a shake of his head. 'I knew it. I suppose that's what I should expect from a hunter. That is what you are, right? Though I don't know what sort of animal you hunt with a Blivet.'

Folly was starting to look very uncomfortable. 'I am a hunter, that's true, but I don't hunt animals.'

'Then what?' asked Vincent. 'People?'

Folly hesitated. 'No, not people. I hunt Supermundane entities – Lurids and Noctivagrantes and Vapids. That's why I carry a Blivet. It's a Supermundane weapon.'

Vincent's mouth fell open.

'It can destroy Lurids, even Phenomenals, and they're particularly tricky – they're so hard to see – but it's a last resort. It's much better just to send them all back to where they came from. My brother is the reason I'm in Degringolade. I was looking for him and the last I heard he'd been seen here with Kamptulicon. I didn't know that he had been hanged for murder.'

Vincent remained speechless.

'So,' said Folly softly, 'now you know.'

Just then the door was flung open and Citrine came running in. She held it for Jonah, who was carrying something rather large and awkward. He set it down on the table with a violent exhalation of breath.

'Look what we've got!'

It was the Cold Cabinet from Edgar's study.

'If we're going to be staying here, I thought we might as well use it,' said Citrine. 'We'll be able to keep food in it.'

'Domna,' said Vincent finally, still looking at Folly. 'That's incredible.'

'Spoken like a true Degringoladian,' said Jonah.

'Not quite.' Citrine laughed. 'Didn't you know? Men say "Domne". "Domna" is for the ladies.'

CHAPTER 31

DUM SPIRO, SPERO

'It's just up here,' whispered Citrine. 'In among the trees.'

It was late Nox and she and her three companions were making their way stealthily across the beautifully titivated grounds of the Capodel Townhouse. The moon, perhaps embarrassed at the chaos it had caused in the early hours of Lux, was hiding behind the inky clouds. They walked in pairs, Citrine and Jonah first, then Folly and Vincent, who were deep in conversation.

'I was wondering,' said Vincent. 'How do we know Kamptulicon hasn't got another bone?'

'It doesn't matter now,' said Folly. 'Once a Lurid has been returned to its final resting place, it's almost impossible to embody it again.'

'Oh, so that means . . .'

'Yes, I can't summon Axel again.' She sighed. 'But that can't be helped. There are other things to worry about now. Kamptulicon won't rest until he gets his book back.'

Vincent laughed softly. 'Good old Jonah, taking

Kamptulicon's cloak. And my smitelight was in there too.'

By now they had reached the copse. Citrine led them into the dense woodland until they came to a small stone building in a clearing.

'The Capodel Kryptos,' she whispered respectfully. In the triangular pediment above the double doors was the family crest. 'This is where Edgar claims to have laid my father to rest today, but I will not believe the body in there is his until I see it with my own eyes.'

'Are you sure you want to do this?' asked Vincent. 'The body was taken from the Tar Pit. It won't be pleasant.'

Citrine nodded. 'I have to know.'

Vincent stepped forward. He handed Folly his smitelight and she directed the light at the lock. Moments later the door was open and the four slipped in.

'Impressive,' whispered Folly with a smile. She shone the smitelight around the cool room.

'It's just like yours,' said Jonah. And it was. There were niches in the walls, complete with caskets and urns, and in the centre was a marble plinth upon which rested a new casket. It was intricately carved, with delicate vines and leaves and flowers. Edgar had spared no expense, noted Vincent. Could Citrine be wrong about the body?

Citrine went to the plinth. 'Will you help me?' she asked, and there was a tremor in her voice.

Vincent stepped forward and flicked the switch on his wrist. Then, using the powerful magnetic force of his artificial hand, he managed to turn and extract the bolts that secured the lid. Even so it wouldn't budge. 'Edgar surely didn't want anyone to open this,' he said under his breath. He admitted defeat and Jonah took over.

Taking his spear, Jonah pushed it between the lid and the casket and began to lever it up. It took all his strength but finally, with a loud cracking noise, the lid came free.

Citrine took a deep breath, steadied herself by holding the edge of the casket and leaned forward.

'Is it your father?'

'Look.'

Jonah and Vincent and Folly all peered cautiously into the gap.

'Sea slugs, it's empty!'

Citrine clasped her hands together and her eyes were shining. 'This means there's still a chance he's alive.'

'Stranger things happen at sea,' murmured Jonah.

CHAPTER 32
LOOSE ENDS

Just inside the wrought-iron gates of the Capodel Chemical Company Manufactory a gleaming black Troika with a trio of horses stood motionless under the night lights. Inside the carriage two men were deep in conversation.

'Well, Leopold, this has proved to be an interesting week – failure and success in equal measure.'

Kamptulicon leaned forward, wringing his hands in the dark. 'But I have proved, have I not, that I can do it? That I can summon a Lurid and give it a body. Is that not what was asked of me? The rest is just a setback, nanything that cannot be dealt with.'

'Well, those four certainly need to be dealt with. But they have gone to ground. Neither hide nor hair has been seen of them since the Ritual.'

'They have something of mine, and I will get it back.' There was a brief silence before Kamptulicon ventured, 'How goes it, down at the Tar Pit?'

The other man sighed. 'The fires are almost out, the Lurids

are still wailing and there's no shortage of tar, so I suppose it's not so bad.' He drained his glass and stood up. 'Shall we go in and see what Mr Capodel has for us?'

Edgar limped to the door – he had taken to using a cane since he had been run over at the hanging – and greeted his two visitors enthusiastically, ushering them into the impressive entrance hall of the Capodel Manufactory. Shortly after, the threesome were making their way towards a set of double doors at the end of a long corridor.

'The funeral went well,' said Leucer.

'Yes, indeed. And now we can continue with our plans. Citrine and her friends can't evade capture for much longer. I have every guardsman in the city looking for her.'

'Good,' said Leucer. 'I do hate loose ends.'

By now they had reached the end of the corridor. 'They're in here,' said Edgar.

He unlocked the door and gestured to the men to go through into the small low-lit room beyond. A gentle hum resonated around the cold space and there was a faint smell of tar. Leucer and Kamptulicon stood and stared for a moment. Behind them Edgar shuffled his feet, rubbing his hands. The Cunningman turned to him with a look of great excitement.

'Domne, but this is splendid! You have outdone yourself,' he said.

Edgar smiled nervously. 'And you, sir,' he said. 'What do you think?'

Leucer d'Avidus nodded his head slowly. 'My dear Edgar,' he said, 'this almost makes up for all the mishaps along the way.'

Edgar beamed with relief. 'Marvellous. I have taken the liberty of bringing a bottle – your favourite, Grainwine. Will you join me in a toast?' He poured three glasses. 'Here's to the three of us,' he said. 'With our combined talents, power and wealth, we are an invincible team.'

And Leopold Kamptulicon, Edgar Capodel and Leucer d'Avidus raised a glass to themselves.

Yes, thought Edgar. I *have* outdone myself, despite all the obstacles, especially Citrine.

And he looked with great satisfaction upon his achievement, one hundred gleaming black Cold Cabinets.

CHAPTER 33

FROM THE *DEGRINGOLADE DAILY*

WANTED

Reported by Hepatic Whitlock

Citrine Capodel	The Rich Girl: a duplicitous, russet-haired, green-eyed, ice-hearted murderess
Vincent	The Thief: a brazen-faced, metal-handed cutpurse and expert picklock
Folly Harpelaine	The Seeker: blonde, leather-clad, versed in the perfidious Furtivartes
Suspect no. 4	The Brute: unnamed as yet, Samson-like, horrifically scarred, violent-tempered and armed with a spear. Do not approach!

These four individuals are believed to work together as a

criminal gang and are responsible for theft, violent acts and murder. It is suspected that they have knowledge of the Furtivartes and are in league with Supermundane forces, as evidenced by Folly Harpelaine's grotesque performance on the shore of the Tar Pit. The Outsider, Vincent, is not a native Degringoladian. The fourth fellow is immensely strong; he assaulted five guardsmen at the Ritual. We cannot ignore the possibility that his powers are derived from unearthly practices. Citrine Capodel's recent escape from the noose certainly smacked of Supermundane intervention. Her cousin Edgar Capodel has disowned her, declaring her no longer worthy of the Capodel name.

Now, dear readers, I do not need to tell you that Degringolade is no stranger to the Supermundane. We all hear the howling Lurids; we take measures to protect ourselves from foul Vapids and Noctivagrantes and Lemures. So you will understand why, in keeping with a long-held tradition in the history of newspapers and for your ease, I have taken it upon myself to name these nefarious criminals. From this moment forward they will be known as:

The Phenomenals
that their reign of terror may come to a quick
and painful end!

'Hmm,' murmured Suma as she handed the paper to Wenceslas. 'Hepatic Whitlock certainly knows how to whip up a storm. To equate those four youngsters with Phenomenals, possibly the most baneful and pernicious of all Supermundane entities? But you know what they say.'

'What's that then?'

'When the local paper goes so far as to give you a name, you've outstayed your welcome.'

Wenceslas harrumphed. 'I suspect these "Phenomenals" will be around a while longer. Methinks they have unfinished business.'

Suma gave him a little smile. 'Let's have a look at the cards. Toss the maerl, Wen, and take a chance.'

Read more **BLOODTHIRSTY, SHOCKING** and **GRUSEOME** stories in . . .

TALES FROM THE SINISTER CITY

F.E. HIGGINS

Look out for another dark and
twisted adventure in

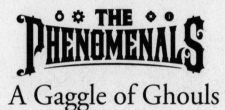

A Gaggle of Ghouls

F . E .   H I G G I N S